Maybe th... ...had the same regrets?

Why would she tell him?

Darcy lifted her gaze then, and the pain in her eyes nearly brought him to his knees. "There's nothing you can do."

If that was the truth, then what the hell. Mack cupped her chin in his hand, saw her eyes widen. "I saw it, too. I felt it, too. Lie to me, but not yourself." His voice was rough in his throat. "Don't think this is easy on me, Darce. It's not." Then, because he couldn't not, he bent forward and planted a soft kiss on her cold lips, lingering for a heartbeat before he pulled away. Now there was surprise in her eyes, and that was better than pain. He ran his thumb over her lower lip, then turned to go back inside.

Because if he didn't, he'd kiss her again. For real. And once they started down that path, there'd be no going back.

* * *

Made for Matrimony:
The road to the altar is paved with true love

Dear Reader,

It's the most wonderful time of the year—but not for Darcy or Mack. A tragedy years ago during the holidays tore them apart and ended their marriage. But now Darcy's back for a final season with her family's farm, and Mack is determined to make her see Holden's Crossing is where she belongs.

I love reunion stories. And I love Christmas stories. So when Darcy and Mack's story came to me, I was so excited to use the backdrop of a Christmas tree farm. For me, one of the best parts of the holiday is stomping around in the snow (or, okay, mud sometimes) and picking out a fresh tree. Yes, they are sticky and prickly and often odd-shaped, but nothing beats the smell of a fresh-cut blue spruce.

I hope you enjoy Darcy and Mack's story this holiday season!

Happy reading!

Ami Weaver

A Husband
for the Holidays

Ami Weaver

HARLEQUIN® SPECIAL EDITION®

Recycling programs
for this product may
not exist in your area.

ISBN-13: 978-0-373-65924-1

A Husband for the Holidays

Copyright © 2015 by Ami Weaver

Printed in U.S.A.

Two-time Golden Heart Award finalist **Ami Weaver** has been reading romance since she was a teen and writing for even longer, so it was only natural she would put the two together. Now she can be found drinking gallons of iced tea at her local coffee shop while doing one of her very favorite things—convincing two characters they deserve their happy-ever-after. Ami lives in Michigan with her four kids, three cats and her very supportive husband.

Books by Ami Weaver

Harlequin Special Edition

From City Girl to Rancher's Wife
The Nanny's Christmas Wish

Harlequin Romance

In the Line of Duty
An Accidental Family

Visit the Author Profile page at Harlequin.com for more titles.

To the baristas at my local Biggby,
who keep me supplied with gallons of iced tea
and a place where I can write without feeling I have
to clean my house. You guys are awesome!

Chapter One

"She's back."

The grim tone of his brother's voice told Mack Lawless all he needed to know, and his heart gave an unwelcome thump. Still, since he hadn't heard from the *she* in question in almost a decade, he deliberately uncoiled more of the pine garland he was hanging on the front of his veterinary practice and kept his voice level. "Who's back?"

Chase moved so he was at the periphery of Mack's vision. Even out of the corner of his eye, Mack could see the tight set of his brother's mouth. Damn. He willed his hands not to shake. He refused to let on that the mention of *her*—even indirectly—could still affect him. He came down the ladder, leaving the boughs hanging and ignoring the sting of the snow that pelted his face. "Chase?"

Chase met his gaze. "Darcy."

Darcy. Her name was a hard punch to his gut. Still. After seven freaking years. He'd gotten over her, and yet…

And yet hearing her name tore the lid off the memories he'd worked so hard to bury.

He forced himself to hold Chase's gaze and not show anything but indifference. "Are you sure?"

Chase nodded. "Saw her at the gas station a bit ago. Thought I'd—thought I should be the one to tell you."

The wind kicked up and the tail of the abandoned garland lashed Mack in the face. He winced, caught it and turned back to the ladder. Mack and Chase were planning to buy her family's tree farm after Christmas. He hadn't thought it would matter to Darcy. She hadn't been back since their divorce, even to visit her aunt and uncle.

His brother angled so the wind was at his back. "You okay, man?"

Irritation flared, but Mack tamped it down. Chase meant well. They all would mean well. As if he was still the heartbroken mess Darcy'd left in her dust all those years ago. "Yeah. It was a long time ago." He fitted the garland over the next hook and pretended the acid in his stomach was because he'd had a burrito for lunch and not because the only woman he'd ever really loved had returned to Holden's Crossing. The woman who'd broken him into shards when she left.

But his damn heart had never fully let her go.

"All right, then. Let me know if you need anything."

In spite of the tension coiling through him, Mack laughed. "Like what?"

Chase shrugged. "Whatever you need. We can talk to her…"

"Oh, no. No talking." He could just imagine how that particular conversation would go. He could almost pity Darcy. *Almost.* "Leave her alone, Chase. I'll deal with her when I have to."

"If you say so." Chase jingled his keys, then walked away. Mack heard his brother's truck start up and forced himself to focus on his task. Now he felt exposed. Anyone who'd seen Darcy, anyone who knew the story—or thought they did—could be driving by right now, staring at him, whispering.

He hated the whispers.

He looped the last of the decoration over the final hook and secured it so the winter winds wouldn't rip it free. Since the weather was steadily getting worse, he opted to leave the Christmas lights for another day. He hoped the wind wouldn't rip them down—the way Darcy had ripped his heart.

He closed the ladder and tried damn hard to ignore the mental picture of his ex-wife, with her long coppery locks and golden brown eyes. Damn it. Now he'd have Darcy on the brain after he'd been so successful at getting her out of it. He forced himself to turn away and haul the ladder back inside, banging it hard on the door. He swallowed a curse as pain radiated up his arm.

"All done?" Sherry's voice was cheery and he relaxed for a moment. His office manager didn't know anything too personal about him, thank God. At least not yet.

"Weather's getting worse," he said as he lugged the ladder down to the hall closet. "Wind is picking up, so I'll finish tomorrow."

She gave a quick nod. "You've had a bunch of calls in the past half hour," she said. "Your family, mostly."

She held the messages out, her attention back on the computer screen.

"Ah. Thanks." He took them and beat it back to his office. He skimmed through them quickly, then dumped them in the trash. Mom. Chase. His sister, Katie. How sad was it to be a thirty-two-year-old man and have your entire family band together over an ex-wife? Had the whole thing really been that bad?

He closed his eyes, then opened them.

Well, yeah, actually it had. Worse, probably.

He stared out his office window at the snow, which had changed from pellets to flakes. The radio station playing in the waiting area announced, between Christmas tunes, that three to six inches of the white stuff was expected by morning. It'd be a white Thanksgiving. Not uncommon in northern Michigan.

Darcy's uncle would be thrilled. And so should Mack.

Mack rubbed his hand over his face. Had Joe and Marla told their niece how he'd been helping out at the farm? Would she have come back if she'd known? He liked them. He enjoyed the labor of trimming the trees, mowing, whatever Joe needed done on the farm. They'd become friends, even with their shared history, but it was funny how the older man hadn't mentioned Darcy's imminent return. Mack was supposed to go out there tonight and help with some of the prep for the tree farm's official opening the day after Thanksgiving. He wanted to make sure this last year went off flawlessly.

Canceling wasn't an option. He knew Joe needed the extra hands more than ever.

Would Joe inform Darcy of the evening's plans?

A small part of him acknowledged the appeal of

showing up and seeing her shocked reaction. Letting her see he was fine and completely over her. He'd moved on with his life. Seven years was a long time and he wasn't that man anymore.

Maybe she isn't that woman anymore, either.

It didn't matter. He didn't want to go there. He'd managed to compartmentalize his relationship with Darcy's uncle away from what he'd had with her. That part of his life was over. At least until now, when it looked as though the past had come back to haunt him.

Sherry appeared in his door. "Jim Miller and Kiko are here. Jennifer's not back from lunch yet," she said, then really looked at him and frowned. "You okay, Mack? You look as if you've seen a ghost."

She wasn't too far off the mark. In a way, he had.

"I'm fine," he assured her. "I'll be with them in a few minutes."

As she exited his office, he sighed and pulled up Kiko's chart on the computer. Kiko was one of many pets he'd see today. Jim and his wife were getting a divorce, and the older man had gotten Kiko, a Siamese cat, as company. Some marriages weren't meant to be, no matter how promising they started out.

Like his and Darcy's.

He filed the unhelpful thoughts away and went to get his patient, whom he could hear yowling from the waiting room. Still, in the back of his head, all he could think was *She's back*.

His ex-wife was back.

Darcy Kramer drove through downtown Holden's Crossing, her hometown until she'd fled after the bust-up of her marriage at the young age of twenty-three.

She'd always loved the town at Christmas. The cheery decorations, the snow, the old-fashioned charm of the buildings added up to magic for a young girl. Somehow there was comfort in knowing it hadn't really changed.

Had it really been almost eight years since she was here? She truly hadn't intended to stay away so long. Shame tugged at her conscience. She knew Mack's older brother, Chase, had seen her back at the gas station. The look he'd given her was far colder than the wind that whipped outside. Had he gone straight to Mack? Probably.

Pain bloomed in her chest. The Lawless family pulled together tight when one of their own was hurt. Except, apparently, those related only by marriage. Those weeks after the accident and the loss of their baby, as her marriage crumbled under the weight of shared grief and her guilt, they'd set themselves firmly in Mack's camp. And he'd turned to them for comfort, rather than her.

She inhaled deeply and forced the memories down. To get through these next two weeks, she had to keep Mack out of her mind as much as possible. Her focus was helping her aunt and uncle, who'd raised her after she lost her parents, with their last Christmas season with the farm.

She gripped the wheel a little tighter. One last Christmas before the tree farm went up for sale. Before he'd died, her father had asked his brother to include Darcy in the final season if they ever sold the farm. So she'd agreed to take two weeks' vacation from her PR job in Chicago and come home.

Home.

Even though she hadn't been here in many years, it was still her childhood home, entwined in her heart and her memories, both the good and not so good. She'd missed being here. But coming back—and possibly facing Mack—hadn't been an option. Until now.

She accelerated as she exited the town limits. The steadily falling snow wasn't yet sticking to the roads, though it was starting to coat the grass. Figured, she'd get up here just in time for the first real snow of the season. Good timing, really. The snow added to the festive holiday atmosphere Kramer Tree Farm prided itself on.

She flexed her fingers on the steering wheel. Two weeks. She could do it. Then she could go back to Chicago and her carefully ordered life. She'd worked so hard for some measure of peace.

She turned on the road leading to the farm. Right away she saw the fences lining the property by the road were faded, even broken in some places. She pulled over in one such spot and got out, zipping the down vest she wore over a fleece jacket to her chin as she walked over to examine the broken board.

The chill that ran through her had nothing to do with the cold. The farm's financial situation must be much worse than her aunt and uncle had let on. Why hadn't he or Marla said anything to her? She'd offered help over the years as her career took off, but they'd always turned her down. She touched the jagged end of the wood, and tears stung her eyes. Her uncle and father had always been so adamant about the appearance of the farm. She swallowed hard as she looked out over the field beyond, with its neat rows of trees. Those, at least, looked well cared for. The wind bit through her fleece jacket and she folded her arms tight over her chest as she walked back to the car.

The farm entrance came into sight up the road and

she turned into the drive with a sense of trepidation. She drove past the low-slung barn that housed handmade wreaths and other decorations, relieved to note at least here the fencing here was in good shape and the area was trimmed festively. There were a half dozen cars parked in the lot and she knew inside the barn would be four or five people making wreaths, grave blankets and other decorations. No doubt her uncle was out in one of the fields somewhere, when he should be taking it easy. The road forked just past the barn, and since her aunt had requested she come to the house first, she continued up the driveway.

The house, a white-painted bungalow with green shutters, already sported lights and garlands and little wreaths hung from wide red ribbons in every window. Smoke curled from the chimney and a sense of relief, of rightness settled in Darcy's bones. When she pictured home, this was exactly how she thought of it. She grabbed her purse and reached for the door handle.

But she couldn't open the door. She'd been gone for so long, for reasons that seemed to pale in light of the farm's plight. Even though she knew she'd done the right thing for both her and Mack, she couldn't stop the wave of guilt that washed over her.

Marshaling her courage, she got out of the car, pulled her bags out of the trunk and trudged across the drive, the snow falling on her face and stinging her cheeks. The weight of her luggage was nothing compared to the weight of the baggage she carried within her. She knocked on the back door and waited. She could see the lights in the kitchen through the curtains, see the shadow of someone hurrying toward the door. Her aunt, of course.

Her breath caught as Marla opened the door, a smile wreathing her ageless face. "Darcy Jane! So nice to see you, honey."

Darcy stepped through the door into her aunt's embrace, letting her bags slide down to the floor. "Hi, Aunt Marla," she said, breathing in her aunt's familiar scent of Jean Nate. She squeezed her eyes shut against tears. Thank God some things didn't change.

Her aunt gave her a squeeze and stepped back. "Let me look at you. My goodness, you don't look any older! You've got your mama's good genes. Come on in, let me shut the door."

Darcy stepped all the way into the kitchen and rejoiced in the smell of pot roast. She never cooked like that for herself. "Mmm. Smells wonderful in here."

Marla opened the oven and took a peek. "I try to have a hot meal for us after these long, cold days of getting ready for the opening. This roast is a bit of a splurge, since you're here. Normally, we don't eat red meat anymore. Trying to keep Joe on a better diet to help his heart."

Darcy toed off her boots. "How is Uncle Joe?"

"He's doing good. He needs to take it easy, which is very hard for him this time of year, but he restricts his working hours and we've got some wonderful employees who pick up any slack. Selling is going to be hard, but it's the right thing to do. It's time."

Darcy hesitated. "I see it needs a little work," she said softly.

Marla nodded. "We've focused on the trees, not that fence out by the road. We couldn't do it all, although—" She stopped, and Darcy could have sworn guilt crossed her aunt's face.

"Although what?"

Her aunt gave her head a quick shake. "Nothing. We've done what we can. Now it's time to turn it over to someone else." She nodded at Darcy's bags. "Why not take those up to your room, honey? It's all fresh for you. We'll eat shortly. I hope you're hungry."

Her stomach chose that moment to unleash a rolling growl. Her aunt cocked an eyebrow. Darcy gave a little laugh. "Guess that's your answer." She'd been too much of a wreck about coming back to Holden's Crossing to do much more than nibble on a protein bar in the car.

"Good thing, too. We've got a lot of food and I don't want your uncle to eat it all. Here, let me help you." Marla picked up one of her bags and Darcy grabbed the last two.

As she followed her aunt to the stairs, she noted the decor hadn't changed much, either. Clean, same plaid couch from when she'd left, same curtains. A large blue spruce stood in front of the big window, lit with hundreds of lights and covered in ornaments. A fire crackled on the hearth, which made the whole place seem homey and cozy.

Sadness gave a little twist under her heart. She'd miss this house when they sold it.

Marla set the small duffel on the bed. "I know it was hard for you to come. I just want you to know how much we appreciate it. And I wish—I wish you hadn't thought you couldn't come home."

Caught, Darcy sank down on the bed. "You know why I couldn't."

Marla held her gaze and Darcy saw understanding and compassion there. "I know why you thought you couldn't. There's a difference."

Darcy dropped her gaze to the quilt and ran her hand over it, the slightly puckered fabric cool under her hand. Leaving gave both of them a chance to start over after the divorce. "Not to me."

"I know that, too. Your dad would be proud of you for coming back. So." She headed for the door. "Come down when you're done. Dinner'll be ready soon. Then we've got work to do."

Darcy stayed on the bed, hearing the stairs creak as her aunt went downstairs. She took a deep, shaky breath.

The memories weren't going to go away. In fact, being here pretty much ensured she'd be assaulted by them at every turn. So she'd deal.

Determined, she stood up and unzipped the nearest bag. She wasn't that naive young woman anymore. She'd been to hell and back. She'd lost her baby and her marriage. There was nothing the Lawless family could dish out she couldn't take.

But she did need to make things right. So she'd apologize to Mack, make him see her intention had never been to cause him any more pain. Maybe then she could forgive herself.

Maybe.

Two hours later, at the kitchen table, her stomach full of Marla's excellent roast, she smiled at her aunt and uncle. "Thank you. That was the best meal I've had in a long time." And tomorrow was Thanksgiving. Two excellent home-cooked meals in a row. Amazing.

They exchanged glances, and then her uncle spoke, his face serious. "Darcy, there's something we need to tell you."

Worry rose so fast she thought she'd choke. "Are you okay, Uncle Joe?"

He patted her arm. "Yes. Oh, yes, Darce, it's not me. It's—well, it's just that Mack has been working here."

That couldn't be right. She clearly had her ex on the brain, because she thought she'd heard her uncle say he was working here. At the farm. Which wasn't possible. Why would Mack be out here? He was a vet. "I'm sorry. What was that?"

He met her gaze. "Mack's been helping me."

The air whooshed out of her lungs. She hadn't misheard. *No. Way.* "*My* Mack?" She winced at her mistake. He hadn't been hers for seven years. "Why?"

Marla laid her hand on Darcy's arm. "He's young and strong. He's been out here for years helping. I know this must be upsetting for you."

She looked away, betrayal humming in her veins. *Upsetting* put it mildly. But they were all adults. What right did she have to expect her family, who lived in this community, to not interact with the Lawless family? "Ah. Well, that's nice of him. I know his vet practice must keep him very busy." She gave a little shrug, trying for casual and fairly sure she'd failed. "Why would it be upsetting? It's been a long time."

Her aunt made a distressed little noise. "Oh, Darcy."

Joe cleared his throat. "One more thing. He's on his way here."

Her gaze snapped to his, panic coiling in her belly. "What?"

Marla looked at her with concern. "He's been out here every night for the past couple of weeks. I know this is a shock—"

"You couldn't have given me a little more warning?" Oh dear, was that a squeak of hysteria in her voice?

"We didn't want to upset you," Marla said simply. "We thought it would be best not to tell you. We talked about it at length, trying to decide how to handle it. Things were so hard for you after the divorce."

She shut her eyes and inhaled deeply, trying to calm her quickly frazzling nerves. Or course they meant well; she didn't doubt that. They were only trying to protect her. Mack, at least, wouldn't be blindsided. Chase would have taken care of that before Darcy got back in her car at the gas station.

"When will he be here?" Amazing, her voice sounded almost calm. Thank God.

Joe glanced at the wall clock. "He's usually here by six thirty. Please understand, Darcy. I know we should have said something before now, but…" He trailed off and looked helplessly at his wife.

She jumped in seamlessly. "But we weren't sure how you'd react. It was hard enough for you to come back as it is. I'm sorry."

Darcy managed a laugh. "I've been over Mack Lawless for years now. If he helps you out, that's great. I've got no problem with it at all."

That wasn't entirely true. But she chose to believe it was because they hadn't told her.

It had nothing to do with maybe not being over him.

Chapter Two

"Well," Marla said as she stood up and began to stack dishes. "I'm going to take care of these and then I'll join you in the barn. Darcy, if you'd rather not go out there tonight, we'd understand."

"No. I'll be fine." She hoped like crazy it was true. She couldn't let her aunt and uncle know how rattled she was.

Marla wouldn't hear of Darcy helping her clean up, which was probably a good thing, as her hands hadn't stopped shaking since they'd told her about Mack, so she got into her down jacket and boots and followed her uncle down the snowy path to the barn. Any other time, she would have found the quiet and the falling snow peaceful. Right now, she found herself too keyed up to enjoy it.

"Finances are a little tight around here, as I'm sure you noticed when you drove up," her uncle said finally.

"Mack offered to help out. He won't accept any pay. Likes the work, he says."

Her heart tugged. That sounded like the Mack she'd known and loved.

"It's okay, Uncle Joe."

He took her hand for the rest of the brief walk and she was grateful for the simple touch. In the workshop, he introduced her to his employees, then said, "We'll be in and out. You remember how to make a wreath?"

In spite of her nerves, she smiled. "I can do it in my sleep, Uncle Joe."

He gave her a quick hug. "Stay strong, honey." He headed outside with his crew and left her alone.

She took a moment to inhale the sharp scent of pine. Some things never changed, and this room was one of them, thankfully. Long scarred tables, open shelves with wire, twine, cutters, pinecones and different colors and styles of ribbon along with boxes of assorted decorations. She admired a finished wreath. It was beautiful—spruce and juniper, with berries, pinecones and a big gold ribbon.

Forcing herself not to watch the clock and failing—just how much longer till six thirty anyway?—she kept busy by gathering supplies for and starting a wreath. Her aunt walked in five minutes before Mack was due to arrive.

"I thought maybe it'd be best if I were here," she said, and Darcy gave her a tremulous smile. "I see you haven't lost your bow-tying skills."

Her aunt kept up a steady chatter, not seeming to expect Darcy to reply, which was good because she had one ear tuned for an approaching engine. When she finally heard it, she took a deep breath.

Marla gave her a sympathetic look. "Relax, honey. It'll be okay."

But Darcy barely heard her as the barn door rolled open and Mack's familiar, long-legged form stepped through. Her breath caught.

He hadn't changed. If anything, he'd gotten even better looking, even in old jeans, boots and a down vest, with a Michigan State ball cap. His brown hair was a little longer, curling slightly at the nape of his neck. He'd always hated the curl, worn it short. Somehow the new style was a sign of how much she'd missed.

His gaze landed on her and he gave her a cool nod. "Darcy. Nice to see you."

It'd been seven years since she heard her name on his lips in that delicious deep voice of his. Longer still since he'd said it with affection, love or passion. Pain and regret hit her like a tidal wave. She'd botched things so badly. She swallowed hard. "Mack." Her voice wasn't much more than a whisper.

Before she could say more he shifted his attention to her aunt. What they talked about, Darcy couldn't say. She turned back to the table to busy herself by tying bows. Her hands shook so hard she kept fumbling the ribbon.

Watching Mack now—because her gaze kept pinging over there on its own—it was clear to her that he wasn't having the same issues she was. He'd gotten over her.

That was good, right? That was why she'd left. Mission accomplished.

Too bad she didn't feel accomplished. She felt torn up inside. Raw.

She started to reach for the scissors when her neck tingled. When she looked up, her gaze locked on Mack's.

Even across the barn and over her aunt's head, she felt the heat of it to her toes.

Oh, no.

She looked down at the bow she'd botched and untied it with trembling fingers. Oh, this was bad.

True, in the years since the divorce she'd barely dated. The few times she'd gone out? Her friends had talked her into it and there'd never been a second date.

She'd never reacted to anyone the way she did to Mack.

"We need to talk."

Darcy jumped at the sound of his voice right behind her. She turned and looked up at him, at the hard set of his jaw, the iciness of his blue eyes. Oh, how she'd hurt this man she'd loved with all her heart. If only she could go back and undo the past.

But she couldn't.

"About what?" Panic fluttered in her throat. He couldn't want to get into their failed marriage already, could he?

"Why we're here."

Darcy put down the scissors she could barely hold anyway and crossed her arms over her chest, needing the barrier it signaled to both of them. "I know why I'm here. My aunt and uncle asked me to be."

His eyes flashed. "You could have come home at any time."

She inhaled sharply. "No. I couldn't. You of all people know why."

"I don't even know why you left in the first place." The words were simple but stark and sliced through her as cleanly as a sharp blade.

She lifted her chin, fought the threat of tears back.

"Of course you do. But it doesn't matter now. I'm going to help my aunt and uncle out, then I'll be out of your life."

He looked at her, his intense blue gaze unreadable. "You'll never be out of my life," he said, his voice low.

Darcy stared after him as he strode out of the barn, his words vibrating in her soul.

Marla hurried over to her. "You okay, dear?"

Darcy forced her lips into what she hoped passed for a smile. "Of course." At her aunt's skeptical look she added, "A little shaken, but I'll be fine, Aunt Marla. It's been a while."

The phone rang and her aunt glared at it, then went to answer, clearly reluctant to leave Darcy alone.

She picked her scissors back up and decided right then not to show how much the encounter had affected her. As she started a new bow, determination set in. It might be too much to hope she could get Mack to understand now what he'd been unable to back then. But she absolutely had to try so she could finally move on.

Wasn't Christmas a season for miracles?

She'd need one.

Mack strode out into the cold, thoughts whirling. He thought he'd been prepared for the shock, but he'd been wrong. Way wrong. Seeing her wasn't easier after all these years.

Especially when she looked so damn appealing.

But it'd been the look in her big brown eyes that killed him—wary, hopeful, sad all mixed together. Regretful.

Regrets. He had a few of those himself.

The still falling snow swirled around him as he approached Joe, who was readying to bale and load cut trees into a truck for delivery at a local store. Joe looked distinctly guilty as he approached.

"You saw Darcy?"

Mack gave a curt nod. "Yeah."

Joe's look was assessing and it made Mack uncomfortable. He didn't want the older man to see how rattled he was. "I'm sorry we didn't talk to you about Darcy. We were afraid you'd quit or that she wouldn't come. We didn't want either to happen."

Mack shook his head. He wouldn't have quit. And he wouldn't have discussed Darcy with her uncle anyway—it would be disloyal and he'd never ask Joe to do that. "It's all right. So where are these going?" He pulled a fresh-cut spruce off the trailer.

"Tom's. Said delivery would be first thing tomorrow." With that, Joe turned the equipment on.

It suited him.

It didn't take nearly long enough to load the truck with the trees and wreaths the grocery store owner had ordered. By the time he'd completed several other tasks and he ducked back into the barn, he didn't see Darcy.

The stab he felt wasn't disappointment. It couldn't be. He'd been there, done that.

He wasn't able to fool himself.

With a sigh, he trudged toward his truck through a good four inches of snow. Joe's voice stopped him.

"Are you going to talk to Darcy?"

Mack turned around. "About what?"

"About what happened."

Anger surged through him, but he forced it down. "There's nothing left to say. It's been a long time, Joe. A long time," he repeated, even though seeing her made it all feel like yesterday. He wanted to forget, to keep it buried. She hadn't wanted them, their family. What good was it to rehash the whole thing now?

"Maybe so. But you two have unfinished business. Talk to her." When Mack opened his mouth, Joe held up a hand. "I'm not going to say any more on this. You're adults. Thanks for the help tonight. We'll be back at it after dinner tomorrow."

Mack said good-night and swiped the fluffy snow off his windshield. He stood there for a second and watched Joe walk up the lane that led to the house. With a sigh he climbed in and started the engine. As he drove back out to the road, exhaustion washed over him. No doubt there'd be no sleep for him tonight. Or he'd dream of Darcy all night. Frankly, he'd prefer no sleep.

He turned in the driveway of his little house, the one he'd bought and restored after Darcy left. He'd needed an outlet for his grief, and this house had provided it. He came in through the front door, and was greeted by enthusiastic barking. Sadie and Lilly came barreling out of the living room and threw themselves at him, barking as if they'd thought he wouldn't be back. He rubbed ears as he waded through them and headed for the kitchen.

"You guys want out?" They zipped to the door and he let them out in the snow in the fenced-in backyard. His phone rang before he even got his coat off. A glance at the caller ID had him bracing himself.

"Hi, Mom."

"Mack. How are you?" There was concern in his mother's voice.

"Fine." And because he was feeling a little contrary with how his family assumed he wasn't, he added, "Why wouldn't I be?"

His mother sighed. "I don't know. Because Darcy is home. And you help out at the tree farm. Did you see her?"

Mack shrugged out of his jacket. "I did." There wasn't anything else to say—at least not to his mom.

"How did it go?" Her voice was gentle.

"I don't know. Fine." He raked a hand though his hair, remembering Darcy's huge, stricken eyes. "Mom. What do you think I'm going to do?"

She sighed. "I don't know. I know how torn up you were when she left. How we thought we'd lose you, too. I know you're an adult, but you're still my boy. And I don't want to see you go through that again."

Mack turned as he heard a noise at the back door. The dogs were ready to come in. He opened it and they tumbled through in a flurry of wet paws and snow and cold air. "It's all in the past, Mom."

She made a little noise that could have been disbelief. "Okay, then. I won't keep you. We'll see you tomorrow."

Tomorrow. Thanksgiving. He'd spent one of those with a pregnant Darcy as his wife. Just before—well, before. It was how he divided everything. Before. And After. He shut the images down. "Sounds good."

She talked a few more minutes and Mack made all the appropriate noises before hanging up with a promise to be on time.

He tossed the phone on the counter and sank down at one of the bar stools lining it. He covered his face with his hands and braced his elbows on the counter. Darcy. All those things he'd worked so hard to avoid were staring him in the face.

He slammed his palms on the surface, and both dogs looked up from their bowls.

"Sorry, guys," he said, and they looked at him as if they saw more than he wanted them to. Wanted anyone to, for that matter.

After a shower, he lay on his bed and turned the TV on, more for distraction than anything else. He flipped through the channels until he found a hockey game he wasn't going to watch anyway.

She'd looked shocked when he said he didn't know why she'd left. How could that be? She'd never told him, she'd just said she wanted a divorce. She'd left in a hurry after that, without so much as a glance back.

He'd been looking for her ever since.

Thanksgiving passed in a blur of fantastic food and frantic preparations for the season opening of Kramer Tree Farm the next morning. Darcy knew Mack was around, but there were so many other people and so much to be done she had no time to dwell on it.

But she was always aware he was in the vicinity. Somehow she was very tuned in to him. That wasn't a good thing.

She hadn't slept so well the previous night, dreaming of Mack. Now, fired up on caffeine and nerves, she figured tonight would be a repeat of the last.

She thought of her quiet condo in Chicago, her refuge from all this emotion and pain. She missed it and the safety it offered—even if it was apparently safety from herself and her memories.

The chatter of the employees, the Christmas music, all combined to make a festive atmosphere. The fresh six inches of snow added to it. Her aunt and uncle were thrilled. She tied the last sprig of bittersweet to the wreath she'd made as Marla came over.

"Looks lovely," she said with a smile. "You haven't lost your touch."

Darcy laughed. "I think I can make these in my sleep. Everything going okay?"

"Yes, thankfully. We're pretty much set. Can I get you to take the ATV out to the warming stations and make sure they are ready to go in the morning? Hot chocolate and coffee out there, and both that and mulled cider up here."

"Sure." Darcy left the completed wreath where it was and stripped off her pitch-sticky work gloves. It only took a couple minutes to gather the supplies she needed and put them in a bag. Outside, she fired up the ATV and drove down the plowed paths to the first—and largest—warming shed. Someone had left the lights on. She parked outside and went in.

Mack turned around, surprise on his face. Darcy squeaked.

"What are you doing here?" she blurted, and realized as his expression closed up how rude she sounded. "I mean—I didn't mean—"

"I know what you meant." He nodded toward the heating unit. "Wasn't running right, so I told your uncle I'd take a look at it."

"Oh. Well. I'll be just a minute." She held up the bag as she edged inside. "I've got cocoa mix for tomorrow. Got to stock up."

She had every right to be here. She couldn't let him intimidate her, not that he was trying. She had nothing to hide or defend to this man. Their marriage was over.

So why were her hands shaking?

When she stood back up, she bumped a can of coffee, which fell off the table and crashed on the floor, leaving a fragrant trail of grounds as it rolled around. Her face burning, she practically dived for it the same moment Mack reached for it.

"I got it," she muttered, then inhaled sharply as Mack's hand closed over hers. His palm was warm, and while she knew she should yank hers back, her gaze flew to his and locked on.

He was only inches from her. His blue eyes were serious and heat sparked in them—and an answering heat spread through her. She wanted to lean forward, just a little and close the gap, see if he tasted like she remembered—

She couldn't afford to remember. She'd spent far too long trying to forget.

"Darcy." His voice was low, a little rough. She swallowed hard and pulled away, gathering the errant coffee can in her arms like a shield. His gaze was shuttered as he sat back on his heels. "Need a broom?"

She blinked at the coffee mess on the floor. "Looks like it." Hopefully, there was a backup coffee can somewhere, or else everyone would have to make do with cocoa. "There's one in the closet. I'll just clean this up and get out of your hair."

She couldn't even tell the heater wasn't working. It was awfully hot in here right now.

She suspected it had everything to do with how Mack managed to kick up her internal temperature.

"You're not in my way," he murmured and retreated to the heater when she came back with the broom. It was as if they were performing some kind of awkward dance. She managed to clean up her mess and stock up the packets with no further incidents, even though she kept sneaking looks at his broad back as he worked on the heater.

She put the broom away and turned toward the door, wanting only to escape the oppressiveness of the room.

"Okay, well, bye," she said in an overly bright tone. "Sorry for the interruption." She made a beeline for the door, unable to resist a last look at him.

He looked up and caught her. "No apologies necessary," he replied quietly.

Darcy escaped outside and took a deep lungful of the cold, crisp air in hope it'd settle the crazy butterflies in her belly.

She didn't care so much about making a mess in front of Mack—though she really hoped Aunt Marla had an extra can of coffee on hand—but her response to him scared her. She'd worked long and hard to move on past the guilt and grief, to build a new and successful life in Chicago. It'd been a long road, and hard won. But seeing Mack threatened all those carefully constructed walls. She couldn't afford that. If she hadn't promised her dad all those years ago she'd be here for this, she'd pack up and leave on Monday.

It wasn't running away when your sanity was on the line. Right?

Chapter Three

Opening day flew by in a merry haze of families and Christmas trees. Darcy was thrilled with the number of people who came out to the farm. The weather cooperated, too, with a very light snow and no wind. She worked the register, greeting old friends and new faces alike. She saw Mack often from her post, as he was helping with tree processing and loading for anyone who needed it. She actually began to suspect there were a few women who didn't need it, but took advantage of the fact they'd get his attention for a few minutes.

She wasn't sure how she felt about that.

She tried very hard not to stare at how perfectly the faded jeans he wore hugged his butt and strong thighs. She also tried to avoid eye contact with him, but it seemed they glanced off each other every time he came into her line of sight. She did note how much the people loved him. Which made sense. As a Lawless, he'd be well-known.

And sometimes she caught him looking at her. Those small moments thrilled her in a way she knew they shouldn't. There was nowhere it could go that would end well.

Only a handful of people alluded to their past and none of them made hurtful comments, even though Darcy had been braced for the worst.

So she was relaxed and happy when they closed at eight that night. Enough that when Marla invited Mack to the house for a hot supper and a drink, she smiled at him.

He accepted without even looking at Marla.

Talk at dinner was minimal, as Marla and Joe were clearly exhausted and they were all starving. But the stew was hot and good and just spooned from the slow cooker. After dinner, Darcy sent them to relax. "I'll get the dishes."

"We both will," Mack said and stood up from the table.

Marla and Joe exchanged a look and Darcy wished he hadn't said anything. Now it was clear what her aunt and uncle were thinking. She didn't want to give them the chance to do any misguided matchmaking.

"Okay," Marla relented. "Thank you."

In silence, Darcy and Mack cleared the table. She was thankful there were only a handful—Mack was doing the suck-all-the-air-out-of-the-room routine that made it hard to concentrate. And he smelled so *good*, like fresh air and snow and pine. She wanted to burrow into his plaid flannel shirt and just breathe him in.

Wait. No, she didn't. She was over him, remember?

She turned the water on and added soap while he quietly got out a clean towel. From the living room, the TV added a nice undertone and helped fill the silence, but didn't do anything to cut the tension.

"So," she said as she slid plates into the sink, "a good day, huh?"

"Very," he agreed. He took the plate from her instead of waiting for her to put it in the drainer. She pulled away quickly. She'd have to be very careful not to touch him accidentally.

"Tell me about your job," he said.

She relaxed. This was a safe topic, not likely to venture into territory she wasn't comfortable with. She filled him in on her PR career, stressing how much she enjoyed it and the city.

Or used to. No point in mentioning the dissatisfaction she'd had over the past few years.

"You love Chicago."

It wasn't a question, almost an accusation. Surprised, she forgot she wasn't going to make eye contact and looked at him. His jaw was tense.

"I do," she said because it was true. She loved the city, the pulse, the vibrancy. The quirky atmosphere.

"So you're happy." The words were quiet, but Darcy recognized them as a minefield. No answer would be the right one. She swallowed hard.

"I am, yeah." She carefully washed the last plate and handed it over, mindful of his long fingers and the memories she had of them, both tender and erotic.

"I'm glad to hear it," he said quietly, and she looked up to catch his gaze. It was sincere and regretful at once. Her heart stuttered. Maybe she could get him to see what had been in her head and heart back then. Maybe she could apologize and he'd accept it. Maybe this was the opportunity she needed to finally move on and find peace.

"Thank you," she murmured, but couldn't look away, gripping the dishcloth because she was afraid she'd reach for him. Touch his face, with the faint shadow of whiskers on his strong jaw. Bury her hands in the longer length of his hair.

Or kiss him.

With a hard swallow, she turned back to the sink. None of those were options. Not a single one. To even think so was madness of a truly bittersweet kind.

He folded the towel and she drained the sink, bumping his arm with hers as he hung it up. She gritted her teeth against the little prickle of heat the contact generated. She didn't want this, but didn't know how to make it go away.

"How about you?" The question was more of a desperate deflection. "How's the vet practice? What else are you up to these days besides helping here?"

He leaned a hip on the counter and folded his arms across his chest. "I'm good. The practice is good. I've got another vet working with me now, too. We're a good team. The practice is expanding and we need more room, so that's why your aunt and uncle are selling to us."

She blinked and went cold. "I'm sorry. What did you say?"

He looked at her strangely, then comprehension dawned. "I'm buying the tree farm, Darce. With Chase. Didn't they tell you?"

She turned to the sink and swiped at it with the cloth,

fighting the sense of betrayal that flooded her. "It must have slipped their minds," she muttered.

What else hadn't she been told? Had things been so bad when her marriage ended they'd tried to shelter her to the point of simply not telling her anything?

He swore, then rubbed a hand over his face. "I'm sorry, I thought you knew. I wouldn't have—"

"Told me. I know. No one around here seems to think I need to know anything that's going on." She sounded put out but couldn't help it. What else didn't she know?

"You've been gone a long time," he pointed out, an edge creeping into his voice.

"I know." The words were bitter on her tongue, all the more so because he was right. "What are you going to do with it?" She wasn't sure she wanted to know.

He pushed off the counter. "Chase has an ecologically sound plan for the place, Darcy. If you stop by my office I'll show you—"

"Wait." She held up a hand. *Ecologically sound* were pretty words that hid a nasty truth. "Is he turning this into a subdivision?" The thought made her sick to her stomach. All the trees leveled, the ponds filled in, the buildings that had been here forever torn down.

"Not like you're thinking, I'm sure. The barn will hold my practice. The rest will be a sub, which will have large lots. The plan is to preserve as many of the trees as possible. It'll be natural, with trails and everything."

The roaring in her ears intensified. "You're taking my childhood home and tearing it down so you can build a subdivision."

Alarm crossed Mack's face as he narrowed his eyes. "You make it sound personal."

"Isn't it?" The bitterness spewed out of her now. "I

hurt you. Badly. I took everything from you and now here's your chance to hurt me back." This farm had always been here, always been a constant in her life. Now it'd be torn down and replaced with houses and people. And no longer part of her.

"Oh, come on, Darcy. It's been seven years! And you haven't been back since to the childhood home you love so much. Your aunt and uncle are important to me. This has nothing to do with you." His voice had risen to match hers, and she glanced at the living room, worried her aunt and uncle would overhear.

She stared at him, the final realization he'd truly moved on hitting her right in the heart. "You knew. And you're still going to destroy it."

"We gave them a fair price," he said simply. "They know my plans. They know Chase's plans. No one's destroying anything. It's why they agreed to sell to us. They had opportunities to turn us down. I'd never pressure them, Darcy. Give me some credit."

The tight edge of anger in his voice forced her to bring it down a few notches. "Right. It's not about me. As long as they are okay with selling the farm to you for a subdivision, it has nothing to do with me." Were her words for Mack, or for herself?

"No, it doesn't." There was a challenge in his eyes. "Because you'll leave. You claim to love it here, but you'll leave it without a second thought. And not ever look back." He snagged his jacket off the back of a chair. "Never mind, Darcy. I've got nothing to justify to you. It doesn't involve you."

His words followed him out the door and she resisted the urge to scream and throw something after him. Tears pricked her eyes and she swallowed hard. He had a point. She'd seen firsthand how little they needed her here, how they didn't see how much she'd loved it. How she'd dreamed of being back.

Whose fault was that? Her own. She'd needed to get away from Holden's Crossing so badly she hadn't thought about what it would mean to relationships with those she'd left behind. Even being in touch long-distance hadn't been enough, though she'd tried to convince herself it was.

It hurt they'd opted not to keep her in the loop. Worse that Mack had been the one to tell her.

Aunt Marla walked in. She looked around the kitchen. "Where's Mack?"

"Gone," Darcy said shortly. Marla frowned.

"Did you two have a fight?"

In spite of herself, she laughed. "Fight? That would imply there was something to fight over. No. He just— he told me he's buying you out."

"Oh." Marla sat down at the table. "Yes. He is."

Darcy didn't have the energy to pursue it further. Plus, it didn't matter, as Mack had made clear. "That's great."

Marla covered Darcy's hand with her own. "He and Chase will treat it with respect, Darce. It's a good choice for all of us."

Darcy's breath caught. *All of us* didn't include her, of course. And now it was too late to ask for a say. Besides, what could she do? She lived in Chicago, for Pete's sake. Her life was there. She'd spent the past seven years making sure everyone knew that. How happy she was, how successful she was, how busy she was.

It had all been a sham.

"Of course it is." She pushed back from the table. "I'm wiped. I think I'll go to bed."

Marla rose and gave her a quick hug. "I'm sorry, honey. We should have told you."

"Just out of curiosity, is there anything else I need to know?"

Marla shook her head. "No. Nothing. Darcy, I'm so sorry for how this has gone."

Being angry with them wouldn't serve anyone. Besides, the one she was mad at was herself. And Mack, no matter how unfair that was. "No harm done," she murmured and hurried up the stairs to her room.

A few minutes later there was a knock on the door. Darcy opened it to find her uncle standing there. "Can I come in?" His voice was quiet.

"Of course." She stepped back. The room was small, and he sat on the bed.

"Marla told me." He took a deep breath. "I know. We should have said something. We've really—we've really dropped the ball when it comes to all this. We thought—we thought we'd kind of ease you into it. That wasn't our intention, to shut you out."

Darcy's mind was whirling. It felt that way, but there was no point in going there. She was as much, if not more, to blame, letting them think she needed to be protected from all this. "I know. I understand." She stared out the window at the light snow that fell, dancing in the reflected light of the Christmas lights on the porch. "But—how can you sell it to them, Uncle Joe?" No matter what Mack said, that he and Chase would keep it intact and not level the whole thing to build wall-to-wall cookie-cutter houses, she couldn't believe him.

Didn't believe him. "It's just—always been here." But of course she could see the proof, that it needed more than Joe and Marla could give it.

"It's been in the family for a few generations now," Joe said. "But there's no one to carry on the farm. Unless..." His voice trailed off and Darcy, hearing the speculation in his tone, pivoted to face him.

"Unless what?"

"Unless you want to run it."

Darcy laughed and slapped her hand on her chest, incredulous. "Me? I couldn't possibly."

Joe's gaze was steady and her laughter died. "Why not?"

She scrambled for an answer. "My life. My job. It's all in Chicago." It seemed obvious. Didn't it?

"Are you happy there?"

She turned back to the window. What was up with that question? Mack had asked her the same thing. "Of course." Wasn't she happy? Was it her guilt that was eating at her?

She heard the creaking of Joe's knees as he rose off the bed and came to stand beside her. When he spoke, his voice was quiet. "As a child, you loved this place. Loved it, Darcy. Followed me and your daddy all over, helping. Even after he died, and you were so young, you kept on helping. With your PR skills, you could take this place and really turn it around. We have a verbal agreement only at this point. No papers have been signed yet."

She stared at his profile, her mind whirling. She had a closet full of stilettos, for God's sake. She'd never wear them here. She was a city girl now. And—Mack was here. Could she live in the same town and still move on with her life?

Joe looked over and slid his arm around her shoulders and pulled her into a hug. She breathed deeply of his outdoorsy, piney scent and squeezed her eyes shut. "Keep it in mind before you reject it totally, Darcy."

She hugged him back. "I can't make any promises, Uncle Joe." She didn't want them to pin their hopes on her. She just didn't see how it could ever work.

She'd worked so hard to make partner, a feat that was almost in her grasp. So hard to earn the respect of her coworkers. So hard to forget what had happened here, to move past it. To come home to stay would be like throwing away the past seven years of her life. Why would she want to undo everything she'd worked so hard for?

Why would she want to face, every day, what she'd tried too hard to forget?

Damn it. It hadn't gone away.

Mack walked into his office Monday morning in a foul mood thanks to his sleepless weekend. Ever since Darcy showed up, he'd been unable to sleep for the damn dreams.

Dreams of Darcy.

They'd managed to spend all weekend together, but not really. She spoke to him when necessary but no more than that. Eye contact was minimal but searing. Sometimes he'd catch her watching him, and he couldn't read her anymore. Wasn't sure he wanted to. It was driving him slowly insane.

Now he went into his office, tossed his coat on the coatrack and dropped in his chair to rub his forehead wearily. God help him, he'd never make it to Christmas this way. She'd kill him all over again and not even know it.

Even though Sherry would fuss at him, he went ahead and started coffee. Functioning on zero sleep required constant caffeine. Delivered by IV preferably. Since that wasn't an option, he headed for the coffeemaker.

There was a rhythm to the mornings. Check everyone, feed everyone, take out those who needed it. Medicine to those who needed it. He embraced the routine today, relieved for the constancy of it. Today he had no truly ill animals, which was always nice. By the time the coffee perked, he was feeling more relaxed.

Jennifer, another vet who worked with him, came in on a flurry of snow.

"Morning," she said, then looked at him hard. "Notice I didn't say 'Good morning,' because you look like hell."

He sputtered a laugh. He could always trust she'd get to the point. "Thanks, Jenn."

"This have anything to do with the return of the ex-wife?"

He shut his eyes for a second before reaching for a food bowl. "You heard."

"Of course. Small town means everyone eventually knows everything." She held up a hand before he could say anything. "You don't have to confirm or deny. Though one look at you is plenty of confirmation for me."

He replaced the bowl and ran his hand down the back of the cat gently. She didn't purr, but neither did she swipe at him. "There's not much to say." He knew his tone was curt but she didn't flinch.

"Maybe I'm not the one you need to talk to," she said softly.

He thought of Darcy, of her laugh, of her spill of hair, of her big brown eyes and smooth skin. Of her cute little body in worn jeans and a long-sleeved T-shirt. Of how he'd thought he was over her and somehow he wasn't.

Nope, no reason to say anything.

"I'm good," he said, and she rolled her eyes at him as Sherry entered the clinic.

The morning passed quickly. He managed to keep thoughts of Darcy to a minimum. He wasn't due to help at the Kramer farm till the weekend. With any luck he'd have this under control by then.

His last patient of the day was a cantankerous old cat. The owner, Mrs. Harris, had known him his whole life, and she still spent most of her days at the bakery she'd owned for as long as Mack could remember.

"Hello, Mrs. Harris," he greeted her as he entered the exam room. "Wolfie's not eating today?"

The older lady frowned. "No. He's just not himself."

An exam of the animal didn't reveal anything untoward, so Mack suggested a change of cat food and sent them on their way with a sample bag. He stood in the reception area, making his notes in Wolfie's chart. Afterward, he ran through the closing duties with his staff and headed out to meet his brother for dinner. It wasn't lost on him how his mother and brother checked up on him regularly. Even Katie had, all the way from California.

He tried to appreciate their concerns, but it was a little stifling.

"So. How's it going with Darcy?" Chase's question was casual, but Mack heard the concern under the words.

"There's nothing to report," he said drily. "I hardly

see her, much less talk to her." All true. She was avoiding him. He knew he should be grateful.

"Mmm. So that's why you look as if you haven't slept in a week," Chase observed, tilting his beer bottle toward Mack. "You want to try again?"

Unsure actually if that question meant change his answer or give it another go with Darcy, he gave the answer that covered both. "No."

Chase raised an eyebrow but said nothing else. Mack stared at the TV, pretending *Monday Night Football* was enthralling, even though he had no idea what the score was and the teams were just a blur, since Darcy's face kept floating through his brain. He rubbed his hand over his face.

"Have you talked to her?"

"Well, yeah. I have to work with her. I'm not going to be rude," Mack said, irritated.

"That's not what I meant."

Mack laughed. "Why would I do that, Chase? It's long over. There's nothing to say."

Other than ask questions. Like, *Why did you leave? Why didn't you love me as much as I loved you? Why wasn't I enough? Why couldn't we pull through our loss?*

And she might have one for him. Like, *Why weren't you there for me when I needed you?*

He had no answer for any of them.

"Nothing to say," he repeated flatly. "Chase. Drop it."

His brother looked at him hard and Mack managed not to flinch. Chase gave a short nod. "All right."

Mack let out a silent exhale. The only way he'd get through this was if people left him alone. All the well-meaning looks and questions were driving him crazy.

He wasn't going to self-destruct just because Darcy was home. Or because she'd leave again.

Because this time she wasn't leaving him behind. He'd walk away first.

Chapter Four

Darcy walked into Java, the local coffee shop, with her laptop bag on her shoulder. Internet at the farm was slow and spotty at best. She needed to check in at work, and this was the best way to do it. She stepped up to the counter, smiled at the barista she didn't recognize and ordered a latte. Then she settled in at a table by the window and booted up her computer.

She frowned at the sheer number of emails. It'd been only a few days since she left, and there were nearly a hundred of them. Many of them from her team on the Grant project. Her phone didn't work reliably up here, either. Apparently the farm was in a technological dead zone. With a sigh, she opened the first one, called her assistant and expected to be putting out fires.

So she didn't see Mack until he was right across from her. She looked up and her heart caught. She didn't hear what her assistant said and had to ask her to repeat. She pulled her computer closer, opening a space on the other side of the table, and gave him a nod. God only knew what this would do to gossip.

When she managed to hang up, he arched an eyebrow. "Problems?"

"I've got it under control," she said, and gave a sharp little laugh. "They take credit for the good stuff, but as soon as things turn into a flaming pile of poo they bail and blame me."

"Why do you put up with it?"

The question stopped her hand in midlift of her now cool latte. Why did she? "I don't know. It's just the way it is."

Mack shook his head. "Sounds as if you need a new team."

She set her cup down. "I've got it under control," she repeated. She wasn't sure why her temper was sparking. Why he'd touched a nerve with a simple observation. "I've worked very hard to get where I am. I'm not going to quit."

"No?" His voice was deadly soft. "Isn't that what you do?"

Her gaze snapped to his, but his was carefully blank. Temper surged, and she welcomed its heat because his words left her cold. "No. I don't. I didn't."

"Sure you did. You never gave us a chance, Darcy."

Darcy's jaw nearly hit the table. "This is not the place for this conversation." She snapped the laptop closed, hands shaking with fury. "In fact, there's no place for this conversation because that would imply we had something to talk about."

"Easy," he said softly. "We're being watched."

Of course they were. She bit back a sharp retort and

slid the laptop into her bag. She offered him a stiff smile. "Enjoy your coffee."

She stood and spun around. Her bag caught on the chair and sent it toppling to the floor. Every head turned, but Mack was off his chair before she could move. He picked up the chair and slid a hand under her elbow. "I'm sorry," he said in her ear as he guided her to the door. She just shook her head, because any words she had for him weren't fit for anyone to overhear. Outside she yanked her arm away and walked as fast as she could in the opposite direction of where he was. Which, she realized after about twenty steam-fueled steps, was away from her car. Which sat in front of the coffee shop. Where Mack stood.

She stopped, shut her eyes, then pivoted. He had his hands in his pockets. He tipped his head toward her car.

She lifted her chin and walked back. When she got close enough to kick him—which was awfully tempting—he caught her arm. "Darcy. I'm sorry."

She looked him in the eye and saw the remorse there. "It's too late, Mack. Sorry isn't enough."

She got in her car and managed to get onto the street with tears burning in her eyes. Oh, no, sorry wasn't enough. It'd never be enough. And she knew that from years of being sorry for how things ended with their marriage. From knowing she could never go back and fix it. Go back and handle it differently, right down to deciding to turn left instead of right.

To save the baby he'd wanted so desperately. When she hadn't been ready to be a mother. She'd barely been ready to be a wife. But she'd gotten pregnant and he'd insisted they marry.

As always, when it came to Mack, she'd been unable to say no.

A sob escaped her and she swiped at her eyes. He had every right to be angry—but she wasn't that young woman anymore. She hadn't been since she lost their baby. She'd grown up in those awful hours after the accident that had fractured their marriage. She hadn't needed him to take care of her. She'd just needed him to be there for her. And he hadn't been able to understand the difference.

He hadn't been wrong. She *had* quit. She'd run away because it was easier than facing everyone else's pain when she could barely tolerate her own.

So no, he hadn't been wrong.

But to hear it from him tore her up inside.

Later that afternoon, Darcy had managed to put the whole thing behind her. Mostly. Now she stood behind the cash register—an old one, nothing electric about it—and smiled at the young couple paying for the tree. They were probably a little older than she and Mack had been, but her heart tugged all the same. Had she ever been that young and in love?

She watched as the husband dropped a kiss on the woman's temple. Oh, yes. She had been. But she'd been uneasy in her marriage and Mack had been so confident. This couple didn't look unbalanced like that.

"This is our first tree together," the woman said, beaming at her husband, who gave her an indulgent smile, then left to talk to Mack, who had the tree. Darcy forced her gaze to stick to the woman in front of her.

"Congratulations," she said a little too cheerfully. "How long have you been married?"

"Eight months." The woman pulled out a check and when she stooped to write it Darcy saw the rounding of her stomach. She saw herself at the same time, the same place and the world tilted. In spite of her best efforts, her gaze shot to Mack, who had his back to her. *This is how we could have been, should have been.*

"Are you all right?" The woman frowned, tore off the check and held it out. "You look awfully pale."

Darcy forced a smile back on her face as she took the piece of paper. "Headaches. They come on fast."

The other woman's face cleared. "I'm sorry. Hope you feel better. Merry Christmas!"

"Merry Christmas," Darcy echoed and watched as she walked to her husband, who slipped a protective arm around her and dropped another kiss on her head. She tilted her chin up to him, love shining on her face.

Longing and sorrow swamped her, hard and fast, and she wrapped her arms around her middle, willing it all away. She'd been so good at not feeling anything for these past few years, and now one happy couple had undone all that hard work.

"Darce." Mack's voice, laced with concern. How had he seen? Where had he come from? She looked up at him, but his face was suspiciously blurry. She blinked.

"I need some air," she said. "Can you watch the register for me?"

Then she bolted.

Mack stood there, stunned as Darcy darted across the barn and into the back. Then he went after her, calling out to another employee to take the register. To hell with this not being his place. Something in her eyes tugged at him and he knew he was helpless to resist. Plus, he owed her after earlier, in the coffee shop.

When he came in the back room, Marla looked at him, then pointed at the door. "I'll get the front."

"Thanks," he said, and went outside.

The cold air hit him with a blast, after the warmth of the back room. She stood by the tree line, her back to him. He saw the defensiveness of her posture, her arms wrapped around herself, her head down.

The fierce need to draw her in, rest his chin on her head, to just hold her, nearly overwhelmed him. He shoved his hands into his pockets instead as he came up beside her. "What's going on? Did that woman upset you?"

Had she been thinking what he had? Seeing them as a young married couple? Wondering how their marriage had disintegrated so fast?

She went even stiffer than before, if that was possible. "Mack, why are you out here?"

"I don't know." It was God's honest truth. He came around to the front of her, but she wouldn't look up. "Darcy. Did she?"

She shook her head. "Of course not. She was very nice. Excited for their first Christmas together." Her voice cracked slightly. She cleared her throat. "I've just got a headache."

A headache. Right. And he'd just grown a third arm. "Okay. Can I get you anything?" Why had he thought she'd maybe confide? That maybe they'd seen the same thing and had the same regrets? Why would she tell him?

She lifted her gaze then, and the pain in her eyes

nearly brought him to his knees. "There's nothing you can do."

If that was the truth, then what the hell? He cupped her chin in his hand, saw her eyes widen. "I saw it, too. I felt it, too. Lie to me, but not yourself." His voice was rough in his throat. "Don't think this is easy on me, Darce. It's not." Then because he couldn't not, he bent forward and planted a soft kiss on her cold lips, lingering for a heartbeat, before he pulled away. Now there was surprise in her eyes, and that was better than pain. He ran his thumb over her lower lip, then turned to go back inside.

Because if he didn't, he'd kiss her again. For real. And once they started down that path, there'd be no going back.

"You going to turn the water off, dear?" Amusement filled Marla's voice as Darcy blinked, then yanked the handle down. *Mack kissed me.* That was a shock after the little scene in the coffee shop earlier. Marla hadn't asked any questions, and that led Darcy to believe Marla thought something had happened with her and Mack.

She wouldn't be wrong, exactly.

It had been a small kiss. A peck, really. But, oh, it— and the look in his eyes—had shot straight to her heart.

She managed a smile for her aunt's sake. "Just tired."

"Mmm-hmm." Marla folded the towel precisely and put it on the counter. "Darcy. What happened today?"

Darcy shut her eyes. She didn't want to relive it. If she'd been able to control the reaction, as she had the few times she was hit with it before, none of this would have happened. Of course, Mack hadn't been within touching distance. "I had a weak moment."

Marla sat down at the table, and the squeak of a second chair being nudged out was a clear hint that she wanted Darcy to have a seat, too. So she did, reluctantly. "Honey, this has been a shock for you. I'm not sure how much you've dealt with since you've been gone." She held up a hand as Darcy opened her mouth to deny it. "Please. Listen. Okay?" Darcy clamped her mouth shut and nodded. "Okay. You left but you never dealt with the pain. You suffered two incredibly hard losses in a short time. You wouldn't talk about it when we asked you. You kept insisting you were fine. And you were so very young to boot. You've thrown yourself into your new life, but reinventing yourself isn't any good if the foundation you've based it on isn't strong."

Tears pricked Darcy's eyes, but she folded her hands tightly in front of her on the table, not wanting to give in to the weakness. Again. Marla's gnarled hand found hers, closing tight over her own. Darcy focused on her aunt's neatly trimmed nails to try to keep the tears at bay.

"Honey. You are strong. You are one of the strongest people I know, and as stubborn as your uncle. You went through hell and back and it's okay to grieve. It's not weak. It's necessary."

Darcy shut her eyes. She appreciated this, she did, but Marla didn't know the whole story. No one did.

"Talk to Mack," Marla said gently. "You don't have to reconcile, but you do have some stuff to put behind you."

Darcy managed a smile. "I appreciate your concern. It has been a shock." That was the absolute truth. Seeing Mack had sent her off-kilter in so many ways. Knowing he was buying the farm had been the least of it. "But there's not much to say, Aunt Marla. It was a long time ago. I don't see what it would change."

Marla sat back and Darcy caught the look of disappointment that passed over her face. She swallowed hard. It was so important that she keep all this locked down. She'd worked so hard to get it to that point. She wasn't sure what would happen if she let it all out now.

The next night, she went upstairs to her room, but she wasn't sleepy, despite her restless nights and busy days. She looked out the window to see the snow had stopped. The moon was shining on the snow, gilding the trees with silver. It was still fairly early, only eight thirty.

She went back downstairs and outside. She needed more shampoo, so she'd run to Jim's to grab some. It'd get her out of her head and off the farm for a little bit.

Win-win.

She drove into town and parked in the half-empty parking lot of the grocery store. Inside, she got her shampoo but stopped dead when she saw who was in line in front of her.

Mack.

Knowing she couldn't turn and slip away once he spotted her, she lifted her chin and got in line.

"Evening," he said, and offered her a smile.

Her breath caught. The laugh lines that fanned out from his eyes added character and were surprisingly sexy. "Hi," she managed to return in a normal voice. Then, because she couldn't stand there and look at him, she dropped her attention to the items he'd put on the belt, including a garish box with a toucan on it.

"Kids' cereal?" A giggle escaped her. "Still?"

He looked sheepish. "Hey. I like them."

"I know." Now her gaze caught his and the weight of a shared past blanketed them for a heartbeat. For once, it wasn't fringed with pain. She swallowed hard.

"How are you tonight?" The cashier's chirpy voice cut through the moment and Darcy looked away, heart pounding, as Mack turned to address the young woman.

She kept her gaze fixed on the colorful box of cereal. Because then she wasn't looking at how those jeans hugged his perfect rear. If she didn't look, she didn't have to acknowledge how badly she wanted to slide her hands over it.

If she didn't acknowledge it, she could pretend everything was normal. That somehow she wasn't losing her tenuous grip on normal.

Oh, who was she kidding? He turned so his profile was to her and she couldn't help looking. He had a small scar on his jaw. That was new. Her fingers itched to touch it, to feel the roughness of the slight growth on his face. He turned to look at her then, and her face turned hot.

"See you, Darcy."

She managed a smile. "Bye."

He walked away, pushing his cart with his couple of grocery bags, and she could still see the box of cereal. It was bittersweet to know some things never changed.

She paid for her own purchase and walked out.

"Darce."

She jumped at his voice. "Mack. What are you doing?"

"Sorry. Didn't mean to scare you." He nodded to the Town Line Diner across the street. "Want to grab coffee? I'd like to make up for the other day."

Oh, yes, more than anything. Which was why, when

she opened her mouth, she fully intended to say no. "Sure."

Blame it on the darn cereal. He looked so relieved, she couldn't berate herself for her weakness. "Great. Let me just put these in the truck. I'll meet you over there."

"Okay." Darcy walked to her car, the butterflies in her midsection going full flutter. What had she done? This wasn't a good idea.

It was just coffee. Maybe a chance to smooth things over.

She sat in her car and waited until he got in his truck, then followed him to the diner. This was why Uncle Joe's suggestion she buy the tree farm was ridiculous. She couldn't imagine running into Mack all over the place. She'd never be able to breathe fully here.

Coward.

Well, yes. Yes, she was. She parked next to him, grabbed her purse and took a deep breath.

She got out of the car and walked in next to him, unable to suppress the little shiver of awareness when his arm brushed hers. Even through the thickness of their coats, she swore she could feel his heat. Neither of them spoke.

Unsettled, she followed him wordlessly to a booth in the corner. She remembered coming here as a teenager with her friends. It smelled the same, of coffee and bacon and burgers. She slipped her jacket off and tried not to look at him.

Which, as it turned out, was easier said than done.

The waitress, perky and young, came over. "Hi, Dr. Lawless. What can I get you?" Darcy swore the young woman batted her eyes at him.

"Hi, Michelle. I'll just have coffee. Darce?" He shifted

his smile from the waitress to her. She resisted the urge to bat her eyes, as well.

The waitress shifted her attention to Darcy and took her in. If she hadn't been already on the edge, she'd have found it amusing to be viewed this way by a girl who couldn't be more than twenty to Mack's thirty-two. Clearly she didn't know the story of Darcy and Mack. If she did, Darcy was willing to bet she'd find her coffee in her lap. "Same. Thanks."

Michelle pocketed her pad and headed off, a definite swing to her hips. Darcy looked back at Mack, whose gaze was on her, not the girl, and raised an eyebrow. "Still charming the ladies?"

"All but one, it seems," he said, and his tone was serious.

She dropped her gaze and toyed with her silverware. He didn't waste time getting to the point. "Why do you think charming her would work?" She meant to keep her tone light and failed.

"I don't. But nothing else does." The frankness of his words caught her. She sat back and regarded him with slightly narrowed eyes.

"What do you want, Mack?" It seemed best to just ask. Maybe they could just clear the air and move on.

He met her gaze as the waitress returned with the coffeepot. Darcy said nothing as she filled both cups, then reached for two creams when she left. "Nice to know some things don't change."

She emptied both in her cup. "Like what?"

"You've always taken your coffee the same way."

The reference to the past, which lately hovered too close to the surface, brought her up short. "I've changed a lot, Mack."

"I know."

"Do you?" She sipped the hot liquid, welcomed the burn. "I've been gone a long time."

"I know that, too." Now his gaze was steady on hers. "We've got a lot to talk about."

She shook her head. "No, not really. Nothing will change what happened and how it was handled. I will say I'm sorry." Damn it, now there were tears burning in her eyes. "I'm so sorry for how it all went down. But it's not all my fault."

He leaned forward. "You left, Darce. Just left."

"No, Mack. You let me go."

Chapter Five

He stared at her. "It was what you wanted."

No, it hadn't been. What she'd wanted was for him to want her—to want their marriage—enough to fight for her. Make her stay. Want her for more than just her role as mother of their child.

He hadn't. He'd just granted the divorce, no questions asked.

He'd never actually asked her why she'd left.

She pushed her cup aside. "It doesn't matter now, does it?"

Mack examined her, this woman who'd once been his wife. He'd so wanted to do right by her, but when it had come down to it, he'd failed her. Failed their baby. It wasn't any less bitter a revelation now than it had been then. He thought of when she'd bolted at the sight of the happy young couple. Clearly, it all mattered to her, too, even if he couldn't get her to admit it.

"It does matter." When she stared at him he cleared his throat. "It matters to me."

He saw regret and pain in her brown eyes. She dropped her gaze. "It was what I wanted."

Even as her words pierced him, he wondered if they were true. But this wasn't the place to push it. He reached over and took her hand, feeling its coldness in his own, but it did nothing to diminish the heat he felt when he touched her. "For what it's worth, I'm sorry, too." For all of it, even the way he'd sprung his plans for the farm on her.

She looked at their linked hands, then gave a nod. "Well, then. Friends?"

He squeezed her fingers before releasing her. "Friends." He didn't think this was settled, not by a long shot. But he'd take these first steps for what they were—a start. At least she wasn't running away in tears.

"So. Tell me about your practice," she invited, and he ran with the topic change, grateful for the chance to just be with her.

Nearly an hour later, he looked at his watch. Time to go back to the clinic. "I've got to go," he said, truly regretful. "I've got a patient to check on."

She looked at her phone, and seemed surprised at the time. "Wow. I didn't realize it was this late. Okay."

They paid the bill and walked out into the cold night. A light snow had moved in and it sparkled in the parking lot lights. Not wanting the evening to end, he turned to her. "Come with me?"

She blinked up at him, snow caught on her lashes. "Excuse me?"

"Do you want to see the clinic?"

He held his breath, not wanting to admit how important this was to him, as she clearly wrestled with the question. "Okay."

Relief flooded him, along with something else he couldn't name. "It's not far. Follow me."

She got in her SUV and followed him to the clinic. He had managed to get the Christmas lights up as well as the garland, and they were lit now—on a timer to go off at eleven, along with all the other businesses along Main Street. Darcy parked across the street and stood there, looking.

He came up next to her, closer than he knew he should. "What do you see?"

She gestured at the street. "It's so cheery. Especially in the snow. When I think of Christmas, this is the scene I picture. I've missed it."

He nearly pointed out she could have come back at any time—in fact, she'd never had to leave—but he didn't want to ruin their new truce. "It is charming." He swept his hand out. "Shall we?"

She gave a little giggle and stepped off the curb. God, how he'd missed her laugh. There hadn't been much laughter after they got married. Then the accident had happened only six months in.

Pushing that thought away, he unlocked the door and reset the alarm. She stepped in behind him, noting the neatness of the waiting room. A Christmas tree stood in one corner, tags hanging off it. "What's this?"

"A wish tree. For the humane society. Things like cat litter, dog food, towels and blankets, that kind of thing. People take a tag, drop off the items and one of us runs it out there."

Oh, yes, this was the man she'd so loved. "What a great idea." When he went in front of her, she took a tag off the tree. "Dry cat food," it read. She slipped it in her purse.

The waiting area had a hard floor, comfy chairs, a few magazines on a table. A bulletin board held pictures of lots of animals and their owners. Another framed picture said "Get to know Dr. Lawless" and had pictures of him and his pets. "This is sweet."

He glanced up from the chart he was looking over. "Oh. Well, people like to see my pets."

"How many?" she asked as she followed him back through a door.

"Two dogs, two cats," he said. "Sometimes more if I'm fostering somebody. Minnie is in here."

She heard the muffled barking behind another door and raised an eyebrow.

"Those are the boarders, or those that are recovering from less intense surgeries. In here I keep those who need a more relaxed environment. Trauma patients or riskier surgeries."

"And who's Minnie?" She followed him into the room, where a little beagle lay on a doggie bed. She thumped her tail when they walked up.

"Minnie was hit by a car. The guy who hit her brought her in. She was— It was touch-and-go. She needs more pain meds."

Darcy stared at the liquid brown eyes, so full of pain yet joy to see them. "Oh, what a sweet girl. Who's her owner?"

"We don't know yet. No collar, no tags, no microchip." He opened the cage door and murmured in a low voice to the dog while Darcy stood back, out of the way, watching. There was a little yelp as he gave her a shot.

Then he rubbed her head as she dozed off. "Here. You can pet her while she falls asleep."

Darcy stepped forward and rubbed the dog's head. Minnie tried to give her a little lick. "Oh, you poor sweet girl. You don't know who she belongs to?"

"No." His tone was grim.

A shudder ran through Darcy. "Abandoned?"

His face was grim. "Happens more than you'd care to know. Foreclosure, need to move, can't take care of the pets. Sometimes they just leave them in the house and walk away. Sometimes they just drop them off somewhere thinking, hey, it's an animal, it can fend for itself. They can't." Anger laced his voice. "I understand not being able to feed them. But I wish—I wish people would bring them to a shelter rather than just abandon them."

She touched his wrist with her free hand, thought of the wish tree in the lobby. "That's so sad. They've got you as an advocate, though. That counts as something."

He moved up next to her, and in the dim light she saw the weight of this on him. The grimness on his face was reflected in his tone. "It's not enough. It will never be enough. However." He reached in, his arm brushing hers, his hand touching hers as he rubbed the now sleeping Minnie's head. "We do what we can."

She looked up at him as he looked back down at her. The heat from the proximity of their bodies drowned out everything else. He was so close she could lay her head on his chest. If she angled her body slightly, she could fit against him, see if it was still as perfect as it had been all those years ago. His hand slid over hers on Minnie's head, and the rough warmth of his palm sent sparks across her skin. He withdrew both their hands together, and his hot gaze dropped to her mouth.

Minnie whimpered in her sleep and Darcy stepped back, her breath shaky, as he shifted his attention to the dog. She cleared her throat. "Will she be okay?" Her words were a little breathy.

"I hope so. So far so good." She heard the roughness of his voice and closed her eyes. This attraction wasn't welcome, yet she couldn't control her reaction to him any more than she could stop breathing.

He latched the cage and made a note in the chart. She stepped a little farther back. "Do you have to come back and check on her later?"

He shook his head. "Jennifer will check on her later tonight. There's an apartment upstairs. She lives there and usually when we have a case like this takes the middle of the night shift."

"Oh. Well. That's handy," she murmured, trying to ignore the completely irrational spurt of jealousy at the casual mention of the other woman. Stupid, and totally unwarranted.

"Yeah, it works well." He tipped his head toward the door. "I've done what I need to here. You ready?"

She followed him back out, noting the quiet with which he shut the door behind him. She nodded toward the other door. "Do they need to be taken out?"

"No, that's all been taken care of for the evening," he said, and set Minnie's chart on the front desk.

"You've done well, Mack." The observation slipped out and he turned to her with surprise. "You fit here."

He moved toward her, his gaze sharp. "As would you, Darcy."

She shook her head. "No, I'm good in Chicago. I love it there."

"Do you?" He moved closer still and she edged back, but the hallway wall stopped her. "Do you really?"

He wasn't holding her in place, but Darcy couldn't seem to move. It was as if her cells had missed him so much she needed to soak up his nearness, his heat, as if he were the sun. She swallowed. "Yes," she whispered.

He moved a little closer and braced one arm on the wall, his gaze never leaving hers, the heat and want there a mirror of her own. "Darcy," he murmured, then lowered his head to settle his mouth on hers.

Her eyes drifted closed and she savored the sweetness of the kiss, which quickly turned to fire as he nipped at her lip. She opened for him and the kiss went from sweet to spicy in a heartbeat.

She slid her arms around his neck and let her fingers play in the longer hair there. He plunged his fingers in her hair and deepened the kiss even more. Fire licked through her, and brought with it the roaring desire she'd always had with Mack.

All of a sudden he wrenched back and left her, nearly panting, against the wall. "God, Darcy, I'm sorry. I didn't mean— I overstepped."

Her face burned. Sorry. Of course he was. "Are you saying we need to just forget it happened?"

He didn't seem to sense the trap. "Yeah, I think that'd be best."

He couldn't have hurt her more if he'd physically struck her. She swallowed hard and lifted her chin. "Well. Consider it forgotten." She darted around him and he let her go.

He let out a curse as the door shut behind her. He'd made a royal mess of it. Not the first time. They'd been making strides toward a fragile peace and then he went and gave in to the need to push her, to touch her, to kiss her. To get her to admit she'd made a mistake. Now she'd be back to avoiding him.

Maybe that was for the best. Maybe they couldn't manage "friends" after all. Especially with kisses like that hanging between them.

He walked back to his office and looked out the window to confirm her car was gone. He didn't want to admit he was more than disappointed she'd left. He hadn't been able to give her a reason to stay when it mattered most, so why did he think it'd be different now?

He was a fool. A fool for Darcy Kramer. It seemed he'd learned nothing over the past several years.

She'd leave—again—and that'd be the end.

This time for good.

Mack had kissed her. Really kissed her.

And she'd melted all over.

The memory of it swirled through her system, like the snowflakes that danced in her headlights. A little shiver ran through her. No one had ever kissed like Mack did, made her feel like Mack did. Not that she had much experience outside of Mack. She'd shut that part of her down.

Of course, he'd also suggested it had been a mistake. So there was that. She tried to ignore the spike of disappointment and remind herself it was for the best.

She snapped out of her reverie when she pulled into the driveway and saw an ambulance parked there. In a heartbeat the panic set in. She threw the car in Park with a gasp and ran up to the door, where she saw her uncle strapped to the gurney and her aunt's ashen face.

"Uncle Joe! Aunt Marla, what happened?" She stood

to the side so the paramedics could load her uncle in the ambulance.

"His heart." Marla turned stricken eyes on Darcy. "He's having pain, shortness of breath, all of it."

Darcy inhaled deeply and took her aunt's arm. "I'll drive you up to the hospital," she said as the nearby paramedic nodded as they climbed into the vehicle. "Let's go."

They hurried back to her still warm car and Darcy bounced down the driveway behind the ambulance. Marla sat beside her and even in the dark, Darcy could feel the tension and fear rolling off her aunt.

Hours passed, and Marla looked up at Darcy. "You'd better call Mack. Let him know."

Darcy inhaled sharply. While she knew her aunt was right, the thought made her own heart beat irregularly. She kept her voice calm. "I don't have his number. If you can put it in my phone, I'll do that now."

Marla nodded, apparently not reading anything on her face, so Darcy pulled her phone out. It was late. Would he even answer? She'd left in such a hurry.

The phone rang twice. Then Mack's voice, low and calm. "Hello?"

Darcy took a deep breath. "It's me. Darcy," she added lamely, momentarily tangled up in the propriety of how to identify herself to the man she'd been married to yet hadn't spoken to for seven years until the past week or so.

"Darcy?" The question he didn't ask was clear in his tone. "Is everything okay?"

"Um, not really. Uncle Joe's in the hospital. Aunt Marla asked me to call you and let you know." She folded her free arm across her middle and stared out at the parking lot, at the snow sifting down on the cars parked there. The coldness of the scene reflected how she felt inside.

"What happened?" He sounded much more alert now.

Darcy explained what she knew. "So it's a waiting game now. I'm with Aunt Marla and some of her friends. They're knitting."

A little chuckle came over the line. "I'm sure they are. I'll be there in fifteen."

Darcy jumped and looked up to see Marla's gaze on her. "Um. That's not necessary. It's so late—"

"See you then."

The phone went dead in her hand and she pulled it away from her ear to stare at it, frustrated. There was no reason for him to be here. They weren't married. Joe was going to be fine.

She walked back over to her aunt, who had needles flying in her hands. She looked up, but the needles never slowed. "Did you talk to him, then?"

Darcy dropped in a chair. "Yep. He said he's on his way."

"That's good." Marla didn't miss a beat. "He'll be a good source of support for you."

"I don't need him," she said, too worried and too tired to care that this conversation had to take place in front of two of Marla's best friends, who knew what had happened with her and Mack. And she almost believed what she'd said. Almost. Truth was, she'd love to lean on him. But the price was more than she could ever pay.

Marla's needles clicked. "Maybe he needs to be here. He and Joe are close."

Of course. Now Darcy just felt foolish. Mack had relationships outside of and independent of her. One of those was with her uncle.

She fidgeted in her chair. The steady click of needles should be calming, but, God, she just hated hospitals. The smell. The feeling. The urgency, the waiting, the memories of a stay here in this hospital, where she'd lost her baby and the seeds of destruction for her marriage had begun to bloom.

Now it had Uncle Joe in its grasp.

She took a deep breath, tried to calm the nerves. Marla needed her to be strong. But it all felt like yesterday.

She laid a hand on her belly lightly, knowing no life beat there. That the last time it had beat there was seven years ago. By the time she'd gotten here after the accident, it had already been too late. And it was possible she'd never get pregnant again. And while she hadn't been ready at the time to be a mother, she'd had the opportunity ripped from her forever.

Of course, being a mother implied there was a man to get her pregnant. A marriage even. Someone who loved her and stood by her.

She thought she'd had a chance at that once, but she'd been wrong, as had the timing. Now that she was older and wiser, she was ready.

But she'd lost the only man she'd ever wanted to share the dream with. Now she was here and so was he and she needed to finally put it all behind her. And forget she was in a hospital and focus on her uncle, who'd need her help more than ever, since he'd be laid up for most of the Christmas season. Which meant what? She'd have to stay? She'd worry about that later.

She was thinking positive. He'd be okay. He was too tough not to be.

But it was so hard to beat back the fear.

Chapter Six

Mack made it to the hospital in under fifteen minutes. Darcy hadn't really said how Joe was, how Marla was. Equally important, how she was. He hurried in and up to the surgical waiting room. When he entered his gaze landed right on Darcy. She sat, arms folded over her middle, her face pinched and white, and stared at the TV, which ran a twenty-four-hour cable news show. Then he looked at Marla, whose expression was knowing despite the tension on her face.

Darcy looked over and he forgot to worry about what they thought.

She'd pulled her hair up in a clip, and pieces had slipped out and fallen all around her face. Memories of the last time they'd spent time in the hospital assaulted him, as they no doubt did her, as well. His gut twisted when she turned her pale face toward him and he saw etched on her face the pain and memories. Not to mention the fear for her uncle.

He crossed the floor but stopped short of pulling her in his arms, though every cell screamed that he needed to get closer, hold her, let her break down and get it all out.

She hadn't let him comfort her when they were married. Why would now, when they were virtually strangers, be any different?

"Mack. You came." It was Marla's voice. Not the one he wanted to hear, but he turned to her and hugged her instead. Darcy wouldn't meet his eyes over Marla's head. Marla hugged him fiercely.

"She needs you," she murmured in a low tone. "She'll never admit it. Thank you for coming," she added in a louder voice.

"Of course," he said, choosing to ignore Marla's words about Darcy. "Any news?"

Marla shook her head and he saw, with a pang, that she looked every one of her years. He'd always thought she was so strong, so youthful. Tonight, fear for her husband had aged her. "Not yet. They said hours, so—" She glanced at the clock.

Darcy came over and rubbed her aunt's back. "Time goes so slow, doesn't it?" He didn't know if Marla caught the undertone of deep sorrow, but he did. He remembered all too well.

"Can you ladies use something from the cafeteria?" He could at least be useful.

One of Marla's friends perked up. "That's a great idea, Mack. Why don't you and Darcy make a run?"

Mack turned to her. She wouldn't like that suggestion, he knew. "Darcy?"

She looked like the proverbial deer caught in headlights. Before she could say anything, Marla spoke up. "He'll need the extra set of hands, dear."

Darcy inclined her head and offered a stiff smile to him. More of a baring of teeth than a real smile. "Well, then. Let's hurry."

She strode away toward the elevator, and he couldn't help watching her slender hips sway. Jeez. What kind of guy stared at a woman's rear when she was worried and scared and suffering from memories better left buried? He tried not to think of her mouth, hot and mobile under his, just a couple hours ago.

He moved after her and stepped into the elevator as she jabbed the button for the basement and therefore the cafeteria. She leaned against the wall of the car, her arms folded tightly across her chest, her stance screaming "leave me alone."

He couldn't. "Darcy." He kept his tone gentle, his stance relaxed. Her gaze shifted to his, then away. "I know what you're going through."

At that her gaze shot to his and she straightened up. "I doubt it very much, Mack."

"You're thinking about that night. It's hard to be here."

"But yet you came," she said, and there was a thread of bitterness under her words.

"Of course I did. Joe and Marla are important to me."

Now her gaze was full of pain. "That's good," she murmured.

He moved closer, trapping her in the corner. "Am I wrong?"

She shook her head. "Not as long as you're here for them only. What went wrong with us can't be fixed, Mack."

"I lied."

She drew back, whether from the words or the heat in his tone, he wasn't sure. He forged on, pinning her in the corner with his gaze, careful not to touch her. "I'm not sorry I kissed you earlier."

She blinked and the elevator door opened. He turned and walked out, sure if he didn't get away right then, he'd give in and kiss her until the pain in her eyes went away. Until the past wouldn't wedge between them anymore.

Darcy followed him into the cafeteria, a little surprised at how busy it was for midnight. But far more shocked by Mack's arrival and his words in the elevator. She'd been working darn hard on a righteous anger and he'd just popped it like a balloon.

She needed the anger to keep her distance. To keep the fear for her uncle at bay.

Right now she was too wrung out to sulk about it.

Mack handed her a tray and proceeded to pile it with crackers, cookies and some fruit. Her hands trembled, but she managed to hold the tray.

He tipped her chin up with one finger. "Hey," he said softly. She blinked back the tears the gesture threatened to break loose. She would not cry, not here, not now, not ever…

He took the tray and set it down, then pulled her in as the dam broke. She couldn't help it, she burrowed in, and he wrapped her up tight, murmuring words she couldn't quite understand, but the tone was soothing. He pressed his lips to her hair. She felt the light kisses even as she sobbed out her fear and anger and regrets into the chest of the man she'd loved more than life itself and had lost.

Finally, she wasn't sure how long it took, but her sobs subsided into hiccups and it dawned on her where she was. She didn't have the energy to break away, even though she knew she needed to. They stood like that, the steady pound of his heart calming her, his heat seeping into places she hadn't known she was cold.

"Better?" His voice was a rumble under her ear. He didn't loosen his grip, but she nodded against his chest and pulled away slightly. He loosened his grip but didn't let her go.

"Oh, no." She touched his shirt lightly. It was wet and sported mascara smears. "I made a mess. I'm sorry." She must look a fright, but she couldn't bring herself to care, even if she was covered in snot, mascara and tears.

He ran his hands up her arms and she became aware they were in a public place, and even though it was late, they had an audience. Still, she couldn't bring herself to break the contact. "I don't care, Darce. It'll wash."

She stepped back and he let her go, with what looked like regret on his face. "Thank you," she whispered, feeling too emotionally flayed to pretend any different. It was the first time she'd cried over all this in seven years. Once she'd realized he was going to just let her walk away, she'd been unable to cry. To grieve what they'd lost. She'd locked it all down.

They paid for their purchases and headed back to the elevator. There she simply stood next to him and drew from his strength. Their arms touched, and the small contact was enough.

It felt good. She'd worry about how dangerous it was another day.

* * *

Back in the waiting room, Marla looked up when they walked in. Darcy knew her aunt took in her tear-ravaged face when her gaze softened. Mack held up the bag and inclined his head toward the cardboard container of drinks Darcy held.

"Food and coffee. Both hospital-grade, but that can't be helped."

Marla managed a small smile at his joke. "Thank you, you two." She glanced at the clock. "Shouldn't be long now."

Marla's friend Carol came over, snagged two coffees and handed one to Marla. "Not too long," she agreed.

Darcy took her aunt a cookie and set it on a napkin next to her. Marla's smile was faint but real. She reached forward and pulled Darcy into a hug.

"Oh, honey. You okay?" she whispered.

Darcy nodded. She needed to address this head-on. "I just had a moment. I'm fine now. You?"

Marla sat back. "I'm hanging in there," she said with a fierce nod. "He'll be okay."

"Yes, he will," Darcy agreed. It simply couldn't go any other way.

She couldn't sit, so she walked back to the window while Aunt Marla's needles clicked away. She held her cooling coffee in both hands and stared at the parking lot. A fine layer of snow coated all the vehicles in the lot. Mack came and stood beside her. He said nothing, just leaned against the wall near her. She decided to be grateful for that. She could allow the small chink in her armor.

As long as she fixed it tomorrow.

The phone rang and the nurse manning the station

answered, speaking in low tones. When she hung up, she said, "Family of Joe Kramer?"

Marla leaped up, Carol catching her knitting as it flew from her lap. Darcy hurried to her side, her heart pounding, her palms clammy. *Please, please, please let him be okay.* She slipped her arm around her aunt's shoulders, felt her take a deep breath. "That's us," she said.

"Come with me," the nurse said. "The doctor will talk to you back here."

They followed her wordlessly back to the room she indicated, where the surgeon was already waiting. He rose to his feet and extended his hand to Marla. "Mrs. Kramer. I'm Dr. Peterson. First of all, let me assure you your husband came through surgery just fine."

Darcy's breath whooshed out at the same time Marla said, "Oh, thank God." Darcy hugged her aunt hard, relief flooding her.

They sat and the doctor went over the details. The upshot was Uncle Joe would be sidelined for the next six to eight weeks. Darcy knew it would make him crazy.

They shook hands with the doctor and went back in the waiting room.

"He's okay," Marla said to Carol, and promptly burst into tears. Her friend opened her arms and hugged her close. Mack came over and stood next to Darcy, but didn't touch her.

"Good news," he said quietly.

She nodded and gave him a wan smile. "Very. A huge relief. They said Aunt Marla can see him soon, once he's out of recovery." She glanced at the clock. "Another forty-five minutes or so, I guess. He's got a long road in front of him, but the doctor was optimistic."

This would mean Joe couldn't work at the farm. They'd need full-time help. He'd check his schedule and see if Jennifer could take over a bit of his load, which would free him up to spend more time at the farm.

Near Darcy.

He wasn't sure yet if that was a good thing or not. Right now they were on fragile ground, because she was distracted—and because the memories that bound them were centered on this hospital. The real test would be when he spent more time at the farm.

"After I see him, you can go home," Marla said. "No point in both of us being here all night."

Darcy sent Marla a worried look. "You can come, too. Lie in your own bed, even if you can't sleep."

Marla shook her head. "I need to be here, Darcy. Please. You'll need to run the farm for now. Can you do that?"

"Of course." Her response was swift and sure.

"I'll help more," Mack said, and watched shock flit over Darcy's face. "I'll work my schedule around it as much as possible. You and Joe don't have to worry about anything but getting him well."

Marla squeezed his hands. "Thank you. I knew we could count on both of you. Don't let it get in the way of your practice, though."

"I won't," he assured her. Darcy looked less than pleased. He'd talk to her later, get her to see his point. They could work around each other just fine. He knew the peace they'd forged tonight was fragile, but they'd have to find a way to make it all work. Put aside the past for the sake of the couple they both loved.

His family would be fairly certain he'd lost his mind. After Marla's visit, and she'd reassured Darcy she was okay now and nearly shoved her to the elevator, she and Mack rode to the first floor in silence.

He saw the worry etched on her face and the exhaustion. "Do you want me to stay?"

Her shock showed he'd overstepped. "Excuse me?"

"At their house. I can sleep on the couch. Keep you company." Clearly, he was so tired his mouth had separated from his common sense. Still, in for a penny...

She blinked and shook her head. "No. I'm fine. I'll be fine," she amended, apparently seeing him forming a rebuttal. "Really."

He bit back a sigh. He had no grounds to push, wasn't sure he wanted to anyway. There were lines, and tonight they'd been grayed out a bit, smudged.

Darcy collapsed on her bed after a tense ride home. Mack had followed her, damn him, reminding her what a great guy he was. She didn't want to be reminded. It was hard enough with the past hovering between them, with the memories, with their loss. All of it combined into an overwhelming emotional morass that she could not deal with tonight on top of her worry about her uncle.

Mack had turned around in the driveway. She was grateful he hadn't tried to talk to her. "Do you want me to stay?" indeed.

Of course she didn't. Not after he'd kissed her and later, held her while she'd cried. He'd been so sweet. Dangerous.

She peeled her clothes off and crawled under the covers, fairly sure sleep would not come for her tonight.

She woke the next morning to light streaming through the window. With a gasp she sat up and grabbed her phone. It was nearly eight. She had to get to the hospital. Aunt Marla needed to come home and sleep and Darcy wanted to know how Uncle Joe was doing. Then she had a tree farm to run. A run through the shower was a necessity and she washed up quickly, ran downstairs as her phone rang.

"Hello?"

"Darcy, it's Aunt Marla."

Dread pooled in her stomach. "Is—"

"Everything is fine, honey. Joe is tough. He's doing exactly what he should be doing for someone postsurgery."

Relief had Darcy slumping against the wall. "Okay, then. That's good."

"It is. Carol and her husband are bringing me home. Did I catch you before you left?"

"Um, yeah. I overslept—"

"No, you didn't." Marla's voice was soothing. "Go back to bed if you can. It was a rough night for both of us."

Darcy looked at the coffee can in her hand. Not likely, but there was no point in saying so. Once she was up, she was up. "I'm good. So I'll see you soon."

"Yes. We're going to grab a little bite to eat and then I'll be there."

A few more words and Darcy hung up. Thankfully, Uncle Joe was okay. Should she tell Mack?

She stuffed the phone in her pocket. No. They'd already crossed too many lines. If he wanted to know he could call her. Or better yet, call Marla.

She started the coffee and poured a bowl of cereal, pulling the books out to peruse over breakfast. She was surprised Marla hadn't strong-armed him into computer records. The records were very complete and organized, but that would have to change— She stopped the thought. It didn't matter now. She wasn't going to use a computer when she'd only be here another week.

The schedule was spelled out in detail. Today she had to oversee the cutting of a fresh load for a big box retailer a couple towns to the south. If they'd had more of that kind of order, maybe the farm would have been okay.

The slam of a car door brought her head up for a moment from the books and her cereal. Must be Aunt Marla. When no one came in and a second door slam got her attention, she stood up and walked to the window.

Aunt Marla was just now being dropped off. So who had come before her?

Her gaze landed on the truck. Oh, no. That couldn't be—could it?

Marla and Carol came in before she could go stomping out in the snow to make sure it wasn't Mack, skipping work to help out here.

Her aunt enveloped her in a hug. Her skin was gray and she looked exhausted, but the little brackets of tension were gone around her eyes. "He'll be okay," she said, and Darcy squeezed her eyes shut against the sting of tears.

"Of course he will," she agreed. Those doctors had better be right. She didn't think her aunt could take losing her husband of so many years this early.

Marla gave her a little squeeze and stepped back. "I see Mack is out there."

Darcy sighed. "There's no need. I can handle it."

Marla exchanged a look with Carol and patted her

arm. "Accept his help, honey. The farm needs it. It's nice of him."

Nice. Darcy nearly snorted. He wanted this place for his own purposes, to expand his vet practice. His brother was going to build houses on it.

Marla slipped off her coat. "Besides, it's going to take some doing to convince Joe to relax and let the farm be managed by someone else. Mack will go a long way to easing his mind."

There was nothing to say to that, so Darcy didn't try. Instead, she pulled her aunt in for a hug. "Are you going to catch some sleep now?"

"She's going to try," Carol answered firmly, and shook her head when Marla opened her mouth. "The doc told you to get some sleep, Marla. Joe needs you to be strong. I promise I'll be back for you in a few hours."

Marla tugged at the hem of her shirt, which was wrinkled. Exhaustion was etched clearly on her face. "I'll try." Then she pointed at her friend. "You, too."

"Me, too," Carol agreed. "I'm going home now. I'll see you this afternoon."

She left and Darcy steered Marla toward the stairs. "Let's get you settled in," she said.

"Did you sleep?" Marla asked.

"I did. You will, too."

Marla paused in the bedroom doorway. "Accept Mack's help, okay, Darcy? I know you'd rather not be around him, but—"

"I'll be fine," Darcy said, and smiled at her aunt. "We'll make it work. Now go. Sleep."

Chapter Seven

Mack looked up from his conversation with one of the employees to see Darcy striding toward him, a frown on her face. He excused himself from the conversation, not missing the other man's interested expression. No doubt this was best done without anyone overhearing. He met her halfway.

"Why are you here?" The anger in her tone caught him off guard, as he took in her flushed face and fisted hands. She wore a green fleece and a red vest, with a red knit cap over her hair. She looked festive. And angry. And hot.

He took a second to focus on something other than the *hot* part of the equation.

"I'm here because your uncle needs help," he said carefully.

She narrowed her eyes and he resisted the urge to pull her in and kiss her. It wouldn't help things right now.

"I can handle it," she said, lifting her chin.

So she was feeling a little territorial about the farm. He got that. "I'm sure you can. But it'll be easier with more help. You've been gone a long time." She stiffened and he guessed that hadn't been the best choice of words. He caught her arm and she didn't pull away. "Darce. I don't mean that as a criticism. I mean that as a fact. You have. And you're leaving before the season is over." And once she left, the farm would be down two people.

Her shoulders slumped a bit, then she straightened back up. "You're right, of course." Her expression was a polite mask, but he caught a hint of pain in her eyes.

He hated to see all the fight go out of her, hated that he was the one who'd done the deflating. He resisted the urge to apologize—for what? For buying the place? For being available to help? "My schedule is pretty flexible. I'm happy to help you guys out. It's no trouble at all."

Her lips curved in a smile that still didn't reach her eyes. "I know my aunt and uncle appreciate it."

"If you are that unhappy about us buying it, you can always buy it yourself." The words slipped out before he could stop them.

She snapped her gaze to his, eyes wide. "No, I really can't, Mack. My life is in Chicago. I can't just—I can't just walk away and leave it behind."

He sent her a sideways look as he started back toward the barn. "Sure you can. If you want this bad enough." His point made, he walked off, leaving her fuming in his wake.

Darcy got the order filled and sent on its way. It was a good thing they had orders to fill. That people came out here to get their trees. It made her happy.

Or would have if Mack weren't about to take it all away. To be fair, yes, it was her aunt and uncle's farm. But how could Mack and his brother look at this place, look at the families, some of whom had been coming here for decades, and decide they could just build houses on it?

And how dare Mack hint that she had a choice? That she could leave her job, leave all she'd done, just walk away from it all?

So, okay, she hadn't been super happy at work lately. She was overworked and stressed, but that was normal for someone trying to make partner as she was. Right? And yes, she felt at home here, even more so than in the city she really did love, but she'd grown up here, so it made sense.

Didn't it?

Damn Mack for making her think. She just wanted to get through all this and back to Chicago. Okay, fine, they were going to tear apart her home. A home that would someday have been their son's—if their baby had lived.

Darcy stopped in her tracks at the thought. She'd never thought of it in those terms before. That the farm would have belonged to their child. That at seven, he'd be running all over, marveling at the magic of Christmas, doubly so on a farm that celebrated Christmas. Something warm hit her face and she realized she was crying. She dashed at the tears with her gloved hands, but they were already crusted with snow.

No. Why now? She'd worked so hard to keep the loss at bay, to lock the pain away. And she couldn't even rectify it—after the accident and the miscarriage, the doctors said she'd probably never have kids. Ever.

Just another reward for her selfishness, and something she'd learned after the fact. Another reason why she'd left. Mack had been so torn up over the loss, but he'd kept saying they could have more kids. Well, they couldn't.

"Darcy. Darcy?" Mack's concern cut through her fog. She tried to ignore him, but he came up behind her. "Darcy?" Now there was concern in his voice.

The snow fell around them, and not too far away, she could hear the happy calls of a family looking for the perfect tree.

"I'm sorry you're upset about the farm," he said, and sounded sincere. "It works well for all of us."

Except me.

Darcy kept the selfish thought to herself and dug though her pockets for a tissue of some kind to wipe her face. Would he think her red face was just from the cold? She could hope.

"Well," she managed in almost normal tones, "of course it does. I mean, you're right. I've been gone. I left. I made my choices."

How could one choice have so many consequences? Over so many years?

"Yes," Mack said carefully as if he sensed a trap. Smart man.

"Okay, then. I've got to—" she checked her watch as if it would give her the answers she needed "—run."

She scooted around him and sent him a wave over her shoulder as she trekked back the way she'd come, hoping he bought her line and left her alone.

Mack watched Darcy flee as if an army of rabid dogs was on her heels. Ah, well. It was better than having her fight with him.

On the other hand, when she was mad, at least she looked at him. And damn if she hadn't sounded as though she'd been crying. But since she'd been so clear on not letting him know he'd opted to honor her. Since his buying this place upset her so much.

Which he didn't want, either. But he couldn't tell her his reasoning. Owning it kept it near him. A piece of her.

Yeah, the fact Chase was going to develop it sucked a bit. But he'd be careful and tasteful. Chase's company specialized in green environmentally sound building practices. It was a big thing up here and, all told, it was much better than some other builder buying it and putting up cookie-cutter houses. Still, he knew it was cold comfort to Darcy.

That evening, he checked in on the animals, even though he didn't doubt for a minute Jennifer was doing a great job. Minnie was doing better, looking perkier and even filling out a little. He stroked her head a bit. When she was healed he'd either find her a new home or keep her himself.

Darcy had been very taken with Minnie that evening she was here. That evening he'd broken down and kissed her, which had been all kinds of stupid, but there it was. Would she like a dog? Or would that not fit in her big-city life?

The beagle licked his hand and he rubbed her ears.

"Everything look okay?"

There was only amusement in Jennifer's tone, and some surprise he'd stopped in here.

"Of course. I just— It's a habit."

"Like tucking in a child before bed, I would imagine." She pushed off the doorjamb as his gut knifed at her comparison.

I wouldn't know. The thought speared him. Jennifer didn't know he'd lost a child. "Most likely."

If she caught the odd tone in his voice, she gave no sign. "It's been as smooth as it always is, Mack."

"Are you saying you guys don't need me here?" he joked, hoping to dispel the tension in himself that had nothing to do with Jennifer and wasn't her fault.

"Of course not." She scratched behind Minnie's ears, as well. "There's always room for a token male."

Surprise huffed out in a laugh. "Damn, girl. You don't pull any punches."

"Nope. You should know that by now." She stepped away from the cage. "You going to fix things with Darcy?"

"What?" He wasn't sure what, if anything, to say.

Jennifer held up a hand. "I have eyes. I can see. The two of you have a lot of unfinished business. I hope she's smart enough to know what she's got in you."

What she had. Past tense. They were long past the point of being able to fix things. To pick up where they'd left off and move forward.

"We're very different people now," he said simply because it was the truth. "We want very different things." He shrugged.

Jennifer made a sympathetic sound in her throat. "Too bad." She turned to walk away. "I'll leave you to your tucking in, then."

"Thanks," he managed as she left. Why couldn't he be interested in *her*? She was smart, funny, cute and he enjoyed her company. She just wasn't Darcy. Not her fault.

He sighed and finished his rounds before heading

out to his house. The house he'd bought for his wife as a present, hoping to cheer her up, to give them a project to work on together.

Instead, she'd left and he'd signed the papers alone. And renovating it had been his therapy. Maybe someday he'd show her. But not tell her the whole story. It seemed cruel somehow, to tie it in with the past.

The house was a small one-story bungalow, white, with a very traditional front porch. He pulled into the drive and up to the garage—he rarely parked in there, since he had to shovel the snow somewhere and it ended up often as not in front of the garage—and got out. The motion light came on as he entered the kitchen. It took a few minutes of blessed busyness to take care of the animals' food, water and outside needs.

He had just finished when there was a knock at the front door. He could guess from all the joy coming from the dogs that it was his mom. She always had a treat for them.

He was right. She smiled at him when he answered the door and petted the dogs, giving them their treats before greeting him with a quick hug.

"Nice that I rate below the dogs," he said affectionately, and she patted his arm.

"Oh, don't be silly. But you don't slather attention on me the way they do."

"*Slather* is the key word there," he noted drily as Lilly attempted to lick his mother's hand while she walked toward the kitchen. She washed her hands and set another bag on the counter.

"So. How's Darcy?"

Mack winced at his mother's question. "Fine, as far as I can tell."

His mother made a harrumphing noise. "As far as you can tell? How can you not know?"

Floored Mack stared at his mother, whose narrowed gaze was lasered in on him. "Why would I know?"

Exasperation laced her tone. "Mack. Because you are working with her. Because you guys have a history—"

Mack held up a hand. "History or not, we're not chatty." He didn't want to explain how trying to reconnect, even tenuously, kept resulting in dead ends. It bothered him. A lot. "We're not—it's been a long time, Mom."

His mother opened the fridge and examined the contents as if all the answers to her confusing offspring resided inside, then turned and grabbed the bag she'd brought. "Maybe you can make it right with her."

Mack frowned. "I thought you didn't want her anywhere near me."

"Why would you think that?" Seeming truly shocked, his mother set the bag back down with a thump. "You and Darcy were perfect for each other. I don't think—" She stopped abruptly.

"Don't think what?" he asked softly.

She pulled out the first container, paused, then turned to him. "Honestly, I don't think she was ready to get married."

Mack's jaw dropped. "How can you say that? You were pushing me to do it!"

She nodded. "I was. But looking back, I see she wasn't ready for any of it. Not like you were. She loved you—I have no doubt about that—but she wasn't ready for the wife-and-motherhood thing."

"She kind of didn't have a choice," he pointed out, even as his stomach soured. Could his mother be right?

She looked at him, her gaze serious. "That's exactly my point, Mack. She didn't have a choice. And before she could even adjust to any of it, she lost all of it. I wish—" She stopped and pressed her fingers to her lips. "I wish I'd seen it then. I wish we hadn't pushed you to do right by her, when it was clearly not what she was ready for."

Mack sat there, stunned. "She could have said no, for God's sake. I didn't force her to marry me." Had he, inadvertently? He'd certainly worked to convince her. Maybe, in retrospect, that should have been his first clue.

She reached over and rubbed his arm. "She could have, you're right. And you were a wonderful husband. If there'd been no—accident, I think you'd have worked it all out and stayed together."

Would they have? As soon as the going got tough, she'd abandoned him emotionally, or so he'd always believed. Now it made sense, especially if his mom was right, and she hadn't been ready.

God, he was an idiot. Worse.

"I guess we'll never know," he said, and heard the note of sadness in his tone. His mother did, too, if the soft look she sent him was any indication.

"Maybe you can start again," she suggested.

"I don't think so." He thought of the pain in Darcy's eyes, and the fierce longing he had to hold her. It was a bad idea. Mack shook his head and pushed back from the counter. "It was a long time ago. We aren't the same people anymore."

"Exactly," she said, so soft he almost didn't catch it. In fact, he decided to pretend he hadn't heard her. Best that way.

Because if she was right, he had to rethink everything he thought he'd known.

Chapter Eight

Darcy ducked into the warm-up shack. Lori, the teenager working, gave her a smile. Christmas music played softly in the background and a fire crackled in the fireplace. The little building smelled of cider, coffee and hot chocolate.

"Hey, Lori. How's it going back here? You got enough cups and cocoa and coffee?"

Lori smiled. "Yep, all good. Been pretty steady back here."

"That's good." Darcy took a moment to check the supplies. "The snow brings people out."

"Yes, it does." The bell over the door jingled and a family came in. Lori greeted them with a smile, and Darcy slipped back out into the snow. It sifted lightly down, as if Mother Nature knew it was two weeks before Christmas and was giving her all to make some magic. Enough to be pretty, not enough to hinder any-one stomping around in it.

Perfect. She walked back up to the pole barn, hearing the roar of the baler, the laughter of kids, the notes of Christmas music here and there. Despite the snow, she wasn't cold. And if it weren't for the fact her uncle was in the hospital, her ex was about to buy her childhood farm—well, no, just for a heartbeat she was happy. In this moment, she was happy,

Her therapist would be so proud of her.

She skirted the busyness but noted the full parking lot as she made her way to the house. Uncle Joe was pos-sibly to be released from the hospital today—seemed a little early to Darcy for someone who'd had heart sur-gery just a few days ago—but he was doing well and Marla didn't seem alarmed, so she'd go with it.

"Ready?" she asked as she came in the warm kitchen. Marla was seated at the table, tying her bootlaces.

"I am. Let's go."

They left the house and got in Darcy's car. She brushed the fluffy snow off quickly, and they were on their way. Darcy followed her aunt to the elevators and tried to breathe normally. The panic was there, press-ing in her throat, but it didn't have claws today. Marla squeezed her arm. She followed her through the maze of corridors. Marla's stride was brisk and Darcy tried not to look at anything as they went. This was not the same floor she'd been on. It wasn't even the same wing.

But it was still the same building.

Marla stopped in front of room 527 and went in. "Good morning," she said, her voice quiet but cheery. Darcy followed her in, and her stomach clenched at the sight of her uncle.

He looked far more frail than he had a few days ago. His hair was mussed—he usually wore a hat from the time he got up until he went to bed—and his skin was pale. He had an IV running from one hand, and the skin around it was bruised and swollen. His eyes were tired, but he smiled at both of them.

"There's my ladies."

Marla went over and took his free hand, pressing a kiss to his forehead, and Darcy saw the look of relief that passed her uncle's face. She came up and kissed him, as well.

"Things okay at the farm?"

In spite of herself, Darcy smiled. He was all business. "Yes. We're moving along."

He quizzed her on a few things and she answered. Fortunately, correctly. She was lucky that she'd grown up on the farm and had retained most of the knowledge from way back when.

He sat back after a few minutes and sighed. Marla touched his hand. "If you overdo it before they even discharge you, they won't let you go today." Her tone was part affection, part exasperation, and he nodded.

"I know. It's just hard. To know I'm missing it."

There was more to that statement than just her uncle wanting the season to go smoothly—more than his need to oversee it. This was the last season and it had to be perfect. And he wasn't there to make sure it happened.

"Darcy and Mack know what they're doing. They've got it all under control." Marla looked at her for confirmation and she nodded.

"Absolutely." Too bad she felt anything but under control since she'd been back here and Mack had re-entered her life.

* * *

Mack was already at the farm when she pulled back in. This was the second day in a row he'd been out here early. She got out of the car and slammed the door, stomping through the snow to the barn. Kelly, one of the wreath makers, looked up when she came in.

"Hey, Darce. How's Joe this morning?"

"Good. Ready to come home."

Kelly's smile was wry. "Marla will have her hands full when he does."

Darcy smiled back. "Yes. She will. Have you seen Mack?"

By now, everyone knew she and Mack had been married. While she didn't talk about it, it had made the rounds pretty quickly. But no one asked her about it, or pressed her. "Pretty sure he went to cut the trees for the delivery today."

Of course he had. "Okay. Thanks."

Kelly went back to work and Darcy went out back. She and Mack needed to have a little chat.

Sure enough, there he was, with four other guys, cutting the trees. She stood to the side for a moment, unable to take her eyes off Mack.

Dressed in old jeans and boots, with an insulated jacket and a hat, he looked right at home among the snowy trees. He didn't hear the approach of the ATV over the sharp whine of the chain saw that felled the trees as if their trunks were made of butter. She pulled her own hat down closer over her ears and came up behind him, the snow crunching under her boots as she picked her way over the drifts to where the men were working. One of the guys saw her and gave a little wave.

Mack turned. As soon as she caught his gaze, her insides heated up.

This was bad. A kiss, and now—now she was worried about being in over her head.

He strode through the snow toward her, his strides long and sure on the uneven path. "Hey," he said when he reached her. She looked up at him, his face ruddy from the cold, and wondered what would happen if she kissed him.

No. She was here to ask him a tricky question. She needed to know. But shouting over the chain saw wasn't the place for this conversation. She leaned in and he leaned down. "Why exactly are you here?" she said into his ear, trying not to breathe in his scent of spice and fresh air.

He turned his head, and his warm breath tickled her ear. She barely suppressed a shiver. "I'm getting the trees ready for the shipment."

She shook her head and he straightened up. The chain saw had quit and the first few seconds of quiet after were almost more deafening in the ringing silence. "No. Mack, you've got a vet practice to run. Really, why are you here and not there?"

His expression turned cautious. "I told you before. Because your uncle needs the help, Darce. I've got my practice under control."

She had to ask. "Are you trying to make up for what happened?"

He stared at her, then frowned. "What happened? With what?"

"You and me."

Her words hung in the crystal-cold air for a second. The sounds of the guys dragging the trees to the wagon, their laughter and voices, all of it seemed to be coming through a kind of filter. Mack's eyes widened and then he frowned.

"What do I have to make up for, Darcy?" The words were clipped and colder than the air around them. She winced when they almost physically struck her, like shards of ice. But she couldn't say anything, because she could see she'd been wrong. Very wrong. "I'm not here for you, not in the way you seem to think. I'm here to help out, because I know your uncle is out of commission and this is important to him. He and your aunt are my friends, Darcy."

"Okay," she said, and turned to go back to the ATV. She'd read something very wrong there. But he caught her arm and, off balance in the snow, she teetered a little as she tried to turn to face him. He ended up with one hand on each of her upper arms.

"What do I need to make up for?" The intensity of his voice made her breath catch.

She blinked at him, the lump in her throat making it hard to breathe. "Nothing." He didn't get it, didn't understand what she'd been through. He didn't see his part in it. She'd made a mistake bringing it up. When his eyes narrowed she pulled away and he let her go. "I'm sorry. I was wrong."

This time when she turned and walked away he let her go.

What the hell had that been all about?

All day the odd encounter with Darcy played through Mack's mind. Over and over. He'd blamed himself for a lot that had happened with them, more maybe than he should have. He'd never viewed working with her uncle as atonement. Joe had never hinted he felt that way, either, so it caught him off guard that Darcy apparently did.

And the upshot seemed to be, it wouldn't be enough to fix—it. Whatever exactly she blamed him for. Looking back, he could see any number of things. He'd failed her in almost every possible way, and no doubt there were more he didn't even know about.

So, no. He wasn't doing this for her. Or for him. He was doing it because it was the right thing, to help out a friend who needed it. It wasn't that he didn't feel the need to make things right for her, as much as he could, but this wasn't the way he'd do it.

He let himself in the house and absorbed the dogs' ardent greeting.

He took care of the drying of paws and dishing out of food, then wandered into his bedroom to take a shower before he scrounged up something to eat. The bedroom he'd have shared with Darcy, if she were still his wife.

That wasn't a line of thought he wanted to follow.

Bone tired, he showered and dressed in sweats and a long-sleeved T-shirt. He waded through the animals to get a container of frozen stew from the freezer and popped it in the microwave. There was a knock at the front door and he frowned, glancing at the time.

He walked through the living room and opened the door to see Darcy standing there, in the dark on his porch. She gave him a tremulous smile and he shoved a hand through his hair before stepping aside. "Darcy. What brings you here? Is Joe okay?"

"Fine," she assured him as she entered, her arm brushing him as she moved past him. "And I won't stay long. I just wanted to apologize."

He closed the door behind her. "For what?"

She shoved her hands into her coat pockets. Her cheeks were pink. He didn't know if it was nerves, the cold or the fact she was too warm in her down jacket. "For my behavior earlier. I was wrong to come after you like that."

The microwave dinged behind him, but he didn't turn around, even when her gaze slid in that direction and back to him. "Bad time?"

"No. Just dinner. Darce. There's no need—no need for apologies." He wanted her to smile, to see her relax. One of the dogs came out and shoved his head against her leg. She patted him with her bare left hand and he wondered what she'd done with her rings. Did she still have them? He had his, wrapped in a plastic bag in the bottom of his underwear drawer. Classy all the way. "That's Sadie."

"Hi, Sadie," she said, her gaze still on the dog, who sat down and looked up at her adoringly.

"Do you want to stay?" The words slipped out before he could stop them. And now it was too late to call them back. "I just reheated some stew, if you're hungry. Otherwise you can just keep me company."

She hesitated. "I'm not hungry. But I can stay a little bit."

After he took her coat, she followed him through the house to the kitchen. He wondered what she thought of it, if he should tell her why he'd bought it. Seeing her wary expression as she seated herself at the breakfast bar, he decided not to.

She looked around and he saw the frank curiosity on her face. "This is really nice, Mack. I like it."

The words fill him with a silly gratitude. "Thanks. I do, too. Chase and I worked on it together."

"How long have you lived here?" She nodded when he held up a bottle of wine. He opened a cupboard and took out a glass, then met her gaze and decided he couldn't do it. Couldn't tell her the whole truth.

"A while now. Long enough to be settled in, I guess." The evasive answer was kinder. If he told her, she'd do the math and realize when he'd bought the house. That might open up more guilt, and there was no point in either of them going there.

He slid the wineglass across the counter and watched as she fingered the stem. Nervous. He seated himself near her and started in on the stew.

"Do you cook?" The surprise in her voice made him laugh around a forkful.

"God, no," he said when he'd swallowed. "My mom makes extra and drops it off. She caught me buying a TV dinner once when I ran into her at the grocery store." He grinned at the memory. Her reaction hadn't been much different than if she'd caught him buying condoms. "She was horrified. And then I started getting containers."

Darcy gave a little laugh. "I bet."

He forked up another bite. "I know I'm too old for my mother to be cooking for me. But she enjoys it. I guess it benefits both of us."

"I guess so," Darcy agreed, a slightly wistful look in her eyes.

"You should come to dinner sometime," he said, and she drew back, already shaking her head.

"Oh, no. After everything..." Her voice trailed off.

"They'd love to see you." That might be a bit of a

stretch when it came to Chase, but after what his mom had said earlier, he knew she would be welcoming.

He wanted to ask her if it was true, if she'd felt rushed into their marriage, then decided now wasn't the time. Besides, Darcy had always been straightforward. They'd talked about it at length when they found out she was pregnant. She'd never expressed any reservations about any of it at all.

She smiled at him then. "Maybe. We'll see."

No, he decided, his mother had been wrong.

The next morning, Marla sat at the table with Darcy. "I need to ask you something."

"Okay," Darcy said carefully, her pulse kicking up.

"I know you only planned to stay a few days." Marla drew in a deep breath and Darcy's heart sank. She knew what was coming. "But. We could really use your help now that Joe is out of commission. Mack can't do it all, since he's got his vet practice. I know he's putting a lot of it on Jennifer, but he can't just leave it. I can't do it all with Joe, and the farm needs someone who can give it attention full-time." Her voice trailed off and Darcy saw the misery on her aunt's face and knew how hard it had been to even ask her.

"Of course I'll stay. I'll make it work," she said with far more confidence than she actually felt. They needed her here, far more than they needed her at work. What did that say about her career? "I need to call my boss and make some arrangements."

Marla grabbed her hands and squeezed tightly. There were tears in her eyes. "Thank you, Darcy. I know—I know there are parts of this that aren't easy for you."

Darcy squeezed back. "You're welcome. It'll be fine.

You don't need to worry about anything but getting Joe back on his feet." She glanced at the clock. "I'm going to give my boss a call and get this all arranged." She had several weeks of vacation. Sad to say, she almost never used any of it. She'd convinced herself she loved her job, and she was pretty sure that was true. But more than that, she didn't have anyone to share the time off with. So really, why bother?

Somehow she'd convinced herself that was okay.

She pulled on her jacket and shoes and grabbed her bag. It'd be easier to do this in the car, without anyone overhearing. She pulled out of the tree farm and drove the little way into town, where she parked in the diner parking lot—she'd noticed earlier her phone signal was strongest there—and hit Ross's number on her phone. It was six o'clock in Chicago, an hour behind, but she knew that he'd be there. Sure enough, he answered on the third ring.

"Darcy. Please tell me you are coming back early." His voice was tense.

Darcy's heart plummeted and she gripped the phone tightly. "What's going on?"

He launched into an explanation of how one of her accounts, the one she'd worked so hard to bring in to the company, was teetering on the edge of disaster. Darcy propped her arm on the steering wheel and rested her head on her hand, the urge to scream building like a head of steam. Why hadn't she been apprised of any of this? Her team was in contact with her, but hadn't said a word. She cut Ross off. "I'll call Mally and talk to her," she said with a calmness she didn't feel. Ross could be an excellent boss, but if he sensed weakness, you'd be out on your tail before you could blink. She'd seen it happen before. And this was why what she was about to ask was risky. "I need the month of December off, Ross."

Silence. Darcy stared at the lit windows of the diner. A couple was laughing, framed by Christmas lights. The woman leaned forward to accept a forkful of something from the man. A simple scene. Why couldn't things in her life be simple? How had she gotten so far off track that she'd lost the simple things?

"You're joking." It wasn't a question. "Your account is going to hell and you're asking for a month off?"

They got the week between Christmas and New Year's off anyway, but Darcy wasn't going to point that out. She kept her voice soothing. The best way to deal with Ross was to stay calm. "My family needs me. I wouldn't ask if it wasn't an emergency."

"Your family needs you," he repeated, and laughed. "Darcy, you never talk about your family. I didn't know you had one. It's why you are the perfect employee. You give me—this company—100 percent. Without fail. There's never any drama with you. It's as if you are married to the company."

Tears stung Darcy's eyes because he was right. It wasn't a compliment. She'd given far more of herself than she'd ever get back. And Ross would take as much as she'd give and come back for more. She knew this, had always known this. But she'd managed to convince herself it was a good thing.

"I need the time off, Ross. My uncle had a serious heart attack and I need to run the business."

"What kind of business is that?"

"A Christmas-tree farm."

A pause, then a bark of laughter exploded in her ear. "A Christmas-tree farm? What the hell do they need you for? Are you going to chop trees in a suit and heels?"

Chapter Nine

Darcy was taken aback by this view of her. Clearly, she'd been good at hiding her past, at making herself over—too good. Not that her boss should necessarily be her friend, but the whole idea that he thought it was ridiculous nettled her. "Of course not. That's ridiculous. I grew up here, Ross. I know what I'm doing and they need me to run it." It was more than a business. It was about traditions, for her family and the families that came to the farm every year. "I wouldn't ask if it wasn't important."

She heard the squeak of Ross's desk chair as he dropped into it. It drove all the employees crazy, that squeaky chair. It was the only thing not full-on chic in her boss's office. Hearing it now, she realized he must have been pacing in front of the windows overlooking Michigan Avenue. She'd bet he hadn't noticed any of the Christmas cheer that Chicago put on, or the beauty of the falling snow. She herself hadn't, not for years, and on purpose. "Darcy. I need you here."

"I can manage my team from here," she said, wishing she had room to pace herself, but the wind outside would make conversation difficult. And stomping around in the slushy mess in the parking lot would ruin her shoes. "I've been checking in with them periodically. And really, Mally is perfectly capable of handling this on her own, Ross. You know she is." Darcy had spent much of her professional life putting out fires before they even reached Ross's radar. Mally needed to do that. Darcy was betting that the account wasn't that bad at all. Now he was seeing just how valuable Darcy was—in time for her to step away. She couldn't help wincing. "I've got plenty of time to take off. This isn't a hugely busy time for us."

It took the better part of an hour, but she got Ross to agree to her time off. She called Mally next and filled her in. Thankfully, the woman was calm and unflappable and very good at what she did. She and Darcy made an excellent team. Mally sounded surprised when Darcy told her she was taking an entire month off, but she didn't make a big deal of it. "Good for you, showing him work isn't the only thing you've got in your life. He tends to think that's how it should be. Probably because it is for him."

Darcy didn't want to be like Ross, so tied to his company he couldn't separate out his real life from his work life. But she was well on her way. It made her wonder—for the first time—if something had happened to send him to seek solace in his work. Like what she had done.

She drove back to the house and sat in the driveway for a minute, just looking. The Christmas lights were on, outlining the house and blanketing the bushes. A huge lit wreath glowed on the side of the barn. The tree dazzled in the living room windows. The whole scene was cozy and familiar and Darcy realized how much she'd missed it. Missed being here.

She thought of Mack's house, the charming bungalow that he'd restored so beautifully. But he had no Christmas decorations up, save a small tabletop tree on the dining room table she'd bet he never used…and she'd double down on the bet that the little tree was his mother's doing.

They'd lost so much, at the time of year when families were supposed to be celebrating.

They'd lost everything.

Darcy swallowed and gathered up her stuff. She'd assumed Mack would move on. That he, wrapped in the Lawless name and family, would be able to grieve and let go and start his life over, without the specter of his very short marriage and almost parenthood hanging over him. It was a huge part of why she'd run.

No, not run. Running implied she'd been unable or unwilling to deal with things as they'd been. But they'd been too much of a mess to fix. She'd seen that clearly. Leaving had been her last gift to Mack, the only way she could see to make it all up to him. Setting him free of all of it.

But—maybe she hadn't. And the thought that she'd given up so much for nothing made her feel ill.

Mack knew he was burning the candle at both ends. Which was why he knew it was a waste of time to stop and grab a beer with Chase. Except Chase was insisting on it and Mack had finally given in.

So he parked in the icy gravel lot of Sloan's Bar and got out, noting he'd beaten his brother here. He pushed through the heavy door and headed up to the bar, where they always sat. This late on a Tuesday, the place was fairly empty. He sat and smiled at Sally, the bartender tonight.

"What'll it be, hon?" was Sally's cheerful greeting. She called everyone hon. He ordered from the tap and waited for Chase. She set the glass in front of him. "You alone or are you meeting someone?"

"Chase," he answered drily. "He asked me to come."

"And now he's late." Sally smiled. "Big brothers, huh?"

"Yeah."

He and Sally had graduated together. She had an older brother, too, but he was in and out of jail. Not really the same.

Chase slid next to him then. "Sorry I'm late." He gave Sally his order and dropped his keys on the bar. "Hell of a day."

"Yeah?" Mack was more than happy to listen to someone else's problems. Anything but his own.

Chase explained how he had a supplier that had first sent the wrong kind of shingles, then the correct ones only to realize they had a major defect. Each delay was more of a setback on a project that was running perilously close to being late as well as over budget.

Mack listened sympathetically. Until Chase cut himself off and said, "What's going on with the tree farm?"

"Going on?" If he played a little dumb, maybe Chase would let him off the hook.

Chase gave him a look and Mack nearly groaned. He wasn't off the hook.

"Come on, Mack. You're spending more time there than at your practice."

Mack folded his arms on the bar and fixed his gaze on the hockey game on the TV across the room. How the hell did he know that? "Joe had a heart attack. You know that."

"Yeah. And you told me he'll be okay."

"He will," Mack agreed. "But not in time to finish out the season. So I'm stepping in."

"Stepping in," Chase repeated. "How does Darcy feel about that?"

Mack took a sip of his beer. "She's not thrilled."

"I bet." Chase dug into the bowl of peanuts that Sally had placed in front of them. "How's it going? Is she speaking to you?"

"Fine. And yeah. We're adults, Chase. All that was a long time ago."

"Mmm-hmm. That's why you've been seen with her around town."

Mack opened his mouth, then shut it and shook his head. "That's not your business."

"When it comes to her, yeah, it is." Chase's tone hardened. "She left you. She wrecked your marriage. She wrecked *you*. There's no way you can go through that again. Hell. No way we can watch you go through it."

Mack rubbed his unpeanutty hand on his face. "Chase. Let it go. Please. She did what she needed to do." The words were low in his throat, almost a growl.

"What she needed to do was stick around and see it through." When Mack's head snapped around, Chase held up a hand. "She never gave you a chance to see if you could go on. To grieve together."

No, she hadn't. And that was something that had

bothered Mack for years. Why hadn't she? Why had she shut down and run? He'd never been able to figure out the answer. "Not your business," he ground out, and Chase gave him a hard look, then sighed.

"I know. But after last time—"

"She'll go back after Christmas," Mack said tightly, and Chase gave a hard nod.

They spent the rest of the time talking about nothing and Mack relaxed. When he went home, he went through the ritual with the dogs and headed for bed, for dreams of Darcy, where she came to him willingly.

But he knew that was all it was—a dream.

Darcy spent a good chunk of the next day on the phone with her team. The good thing was, Ross's interpretation of the situation was wrong, which relieved Darcy. Mally had it all well in hand, which she'd already determined from their conversation yesterday. They agreed to stay in touch with emails and calls every other day, unless Mally needed more. Darcy didn't think she would.

Mack's truck, which had been there earlier in the day, was gone when she got back to the farm. No doubt he'd gone to his real job.

She wished she could make him see that she had this under control. That while his help was appreciated, she didn't need him to come every day for ten hours. He didn't have to give anything up for her. For them. For whoever.

He was stubborn. She knew this all too well.

She dropped her laptop off in the house, got her winter stuff on and trudged over to the barn. They didn't open until three on weekdays, so she had a little time.

She checked the wreath orders when she was in there, and started making another one. They had four due to be picked up today, and a few more the next day. This was a part she'd like to expand. The wreath making, the grave blankets, the garlands, all the piney decorations.

Of course, it didn't matter now. This was the end of the road for the tree farm, and thinking of ideas now didn't help. Why hadn't she made the suggestions before now?

Because you hadn't known. You should have known.

And that was a loop that had played in her mind over and over since she came back. It was pointless and frustrating. And maybe wouldn't have made any difference after all. Her aunt and uncle were selling because it was time to move on. Not because of anything she'd done, or not. She couldn't prevent them from aging or retiring.

But the guilt sat heavily in her chest as she went through the motions of making a wreath.

You should have known.

"Darcy." Marla looked up with a smile when she came into the house. Joe sat at the table, still looking pale, but far better than he had been. Recovery was taking a while, but he was getting there.

"How's it going out there?" Joe's question was casual, but the slight tension in his body gave away how much he missed being in the action.

"Just fine," Darcy said. She put the paper with the notes she took in front of him. It had the sales on it and other information he just devoured. It was a kind of unspoken compromise. He'd stay in the house and she'd give him the information he wanted.

Marla held out a carefully packed casserole. "Can

you take this to Mack? I told him I'd be by but—" she glanced at the clock "—I'm not going to get over there before my book club comes over."

Caught, Darcy took the pan. There was no way to say no. "Of course. I'll get right on that."

"Thanks," Marla said gratefully, and untied her apron. "I've got about fifteen minutes."

Darcy was about to ask why she was hosting it, at this time of year, but then she realized of course Marla wasn't going to leave Joe alone. And her friends would understand that.

She went back out the door to her car and drove to Mack's. This time, the porch light was on. She parked on the street and went up the front walk. She knocked and realized that she hadn't asked if Mack knew she was coming.

When he answered the door, his warm smile slipping into clear shock that she was standing there, she had her answer. "Marla couldn't make it," she said, holding out the packages. "She ran out of time. So she sent me instead." This was stating the obvious and she felt a little silly. She was always so off-kilter around him.

He stepped back. "Come on in."

"Oh, I can't stay," she said, and found herself stepping into the warm house anyway.

"I'm sure there's enough for both of us," he said wryly. She wondered if it was what Marla had in mind. Now that she thought about it, she wouldn't put it past her aunt. "Sure," she said, and took off her coat, then followed him into the kitchen. This house was big for a bachelor. Unless—

"Mack, do you have a girlfriend?"

The question was out before she could stop it. He

dropped the silverware he'd just pulled out of the drawer. "What the hell kind of question is that?" He stepped over the pieces on the floor and came over to her, the look on his face completely predatory. "Do you think, if I had a girlfriend, I'd do this with you?" And his mouth came down on hers.

It wasn't a gentle kiss. It was an angry kiss, a punishing kiss. A kiss that shot to her soul and flared to life.

She needed to stop it, to push him away. Instead, she wound her arms around his neck and kissed him back, all the hunger and need she'd felt since she came home—probably well before that—pouring out of her. When he backed her into the fridge, she welcomed the hard press of his body, the way his hands fisted in her hair and his mouth plundered hers.

When he pulled back, the loudest sound in the room was that of their ragged breathing. "Does that answer your question?" His voice was rough, and the sound made shivers skip over her skin.

For a moment, she couldn't recall the question.

"Yes," she managed, when the fog cleared enough for her to think. "It does." But it opened up more questions, the biggest one of which was *why?* Why had he kissed her? Why did he still care? Why did she?

Those weren't questions she could answer. That she *wanted* to answer.

"So I guess I'll leave you to dinner," she said, and edged for the door.

He looked at her, his eyes still smoky with desire and want and need. "Running away?"

She stopped, affronted, but couldn't make herself meet his gaze. "What? No, of course not."

"Are you sure?" He stepped closer. "You were will-ing to stay until I kissed you."

Caught, she just looked at him, afraid of what he might see, of what she wasn't ready for him to see. Of what she wasn't ready to admit to herself. She tucked her hair behind her ear.

"I'll behave," he said, and the wicked tilt to his mouth made her raise an eyebrow. "Scout's honor."

Now she lifted both eyebrows. "Were you ever a Scout?"

"No," he admitted. "But Chase was."

"All right," she relented, and moved back toward the island. She didn't really want to leave. "Anything I can do?"

He directed her to the glasses and she got out new silverware, placing the pieces that had been on the floor in the sink. It didn't take long to get the simple meal on the table—and Darcy would bet that her aunt had planned this. Book club, dinner, send her out to run the errand—it had Marla's fingerprints all over it.

Darcy couldn't be mad.

They sat at the table, and she refrained from asking him how often he used it. There was a cozy bay window overlooking the backyard, and while it was too dark to really see anything out there, she could tell it had begun to snow. "That's a real tree?" she asked, nodding toward the one on the table.

"It is," he agreed, and took a bite of his dinner.

"Why not have a full-size tree?"

He looked at her as if she'd grown an extra head. "Why would I do that?"

"You work at a Christmas-tree farm," she pointed out. "Surely you could get one there."

He gave her a wry, almost sad, smile. "No need. It's just me. I don't get trees anymore."

Anymore. The implication of that hit her hard. Of course he didn't. When was the last time she'd gotten one? Her last tree, other than a little halfhearted, fake formal tree she did just because she felt she had to, had been here. With Mack.

Oh, no.

"We need to fix that." She couldn't do much to fix the past or her mistakes, but she could give him this. It was a little thing, a small thing, but a start.

"We do? Why?" He sounded truly puzzled.

"Because it's not right. You should have a tree. This house should have a tree."

"Darcy—"

"I happen to know the owner of a tree farm." She offered him a crooked smile. "I think I can get you in."

Damn if he could resist her. "Darce. I don't have any ornaments." That wasn't completely true. He had the boxes of the ones they'd picked out together, all those years ago. His mother had packed them up for him, when he was unable to face anything, much less packing up a Christmas tree. He'd never touched them since. They were in her attic. That wouldn't work.

"That's okay. We can get some. I'm sure there are extras in Marla and Joe's attic."

He carried his plate to the sink and she followed. "When did you want to do this?"

"Now?"

He looked over her head at the microwave clock. "It's eight thirty. The farm's closed."

She shrugged. "That's what flashlights are for."

What the hell? "All right. Let me get my stuff on."

He followed her to the farm. The snow was coming down lightly, a sifting that glittered in the headlights. They both parked by the barn, not the house. She already had on her boots and parka and hat and gloves. She gave him a smile in the light of the big wreath on the front of the barn. "Ready?"

For a guy who hadn't bothered with Christmas since his wife left him—a wife who was standing in front of him now—he was remarkably ready. "Let's go."

He grabbed a saw and she got the flashlight and a cart to haul the tree up to his truck. They walked down the lane, the silence broken by the creak of the wagon wheels, the crunch of their boots on the packed snow and, if they stopped moving, the sound of the snow collecting on the branches around them.

"Spruce?" she asked as they stopped at a fork in the lane. Her breath puffed out in front of her in the cold.

"What else?"

She inclined her head in acknowledgment and turned to the left. She stopped a few feet down and dropped the handle of the wagon. Trying to drag it through the snow would be too much work. "How big?"

He followed her, amused, and still able to pick out the sway of her hips even in the dark. The metallic finish of her blue coat caught the beam of the flashlight. "Six feet or so. Pretty full."

She aimed the light at him, momentarily blinding him. "Oh, sorry! Are you okay? And have a little faith, okay?"

He'd lost what little faith he had left when she left him. But now wasn't the time to tell her that. Not when things were going well with them. Whatever *things* were.

It took some time, and he enjoyed stomping around

in the dark with her. She finally settled on a tree that was tall enough and fairly full. "This one okay?"

He took the light from her and flashed it over it. He couldn't resist teasing her a little bit. "Looks good to me. But of course, it's dark out, Darce."

She snatched the light back. "It's fine."

He caught her chin in his hand and pressed a kiss to her cold lips. He couldn't help it. Being out here in the dark and cold, with the sharp scent of pine and the softly sifting snow, made him miss her more. Want her more. When he pulled back, looking in her eyes, even in the dark he could see the desire there. When she breathed his name on puff of peppermint-scented air, he was lost.

This kiss was sweet, bittersweet. He knew they were going down a path that was going to end up in heart-break for both of them—well, him for sure. Then she dropped the heavy metal flashlight on the top of his foot.

"Sorry," she said sheepishly. "I forgot I had it."

He kissed her forehead. "Good thing my boots are thick. Next time you want me to stop kissing you, just tell me instead of trying to hurt me, okay?"

He was teasing, but only sort of. She fished the light out of the snow and he went over to saw the tree down.

By the time they got it back to his truck, he was cold and wet, but it was worth every minute of her company. "Do you want to come in?" She jerked her head toward the house. "Get something to warm you up?"

Tempting as it was— "No. I'm going to go home and change out of these wet clothes. I'll see you tomorrow."

Disappointment flashed over her face. "All right. Tomorrow we'll get the lights on it."

"Sounds good."

He drove away, seeing her in the red glow of his tail-lights as he went back up the lane to the main road, the tree bouncing in the bed of the truck.

Chapter Ten

Darcy wasn't sure what had come over her the night before. Mack's kisses were seared in her brain, and about all she could come up with was she had somehow fallen back into the past. A time warp of sorts, triggered somehow by being in his presence. For a few minutes it'd almost been as if nothing had happened.

In the early days of their marriage, there'd been no hot kisses like that. Oh, they'd been the ones that had gotten them in trouble. Her pregnancy had meant they'd had to get married. He'd insisted on doing the right thing, and since she couldn't see herself with anyone else—even if she wasn't totally sure she wanted to get married yet—she'd gone along. He'd been happy.

But she hadn't been.

How bad was that? He'd been so sure. She'd allowed him to sweep her off her feet. But then her worst fears had been realized. He only wanted her as long as the baby was in the picture. She, by herself, hadn't been enough. So how had she gotten all caught up in it again?

Her phone rang and Darcy tucked the phone on her shoulder as she answered. "Hi, Corrie."

"Darcy! I miss you, girl. How is it way up there?"

Darcy curled up in the chair and smiled at her best friend's exuberant greeting. "Same as it always is. Cold." Her hands and lips were a little chapped.

"Mmm. How's the ex-husband?"

Just like Corrie to cut right to the heart of the matter. Darcy stared into the flames, which crackled cheerily around the logs she'd added just before the phone rang. "Fine."

"Fine," Corrie repeated. "That tells me nothing."

"That's because there's nothing to tell," Darcy said, trying to keep her voice light. She knew she'd failed when she heard Corrie's sigh.

"Darcy. Come on. Is he hot? Or did he get sloppy?"

"Hot," she answered before she could stop herself.

A long pause. Darcy shut her eyes. She'd stepped in it now.

"Really?" Corrie drew out the word. "That's pretty definitive, Darce. You still have feelings for him."

It wasn't a question, but Darcy chose to treat it as one. "No. No more than nostalgia. We were married, Corrie. That carries some weight, even after all these years." Or so she'd been trying to convince herself. That it was all just based on where they'd been.

"Would it be so bad? If there were feelings between you two? You've shut yourself down pretty tight, Darce. Seems like getting the opportunity to move on would be good for you. Even if it's moving on with him."

She laughed, because if she didn't, she'd cry. "It'd be

awful. I can't stay here. You know that. There's nothing for me here. And Mack—well, he was pretty clear all those years ago it was over. I'm not willing to give it a shot. Plus, there's no time." And thank God for it. She wasn't risking her heart, not with the guy who'd broken it in the first place.

"If you say so," Corrie said softly. "But, Darcy. Promise me you'll keep your options open. Just in case."

Darcy shook her head and pressed her fingers to her lips, even though her friend couldn't see her. "I can't. You of all people know that." Mack hadn't understood then. Why would he now? She wasn't going to risk her heart on that. She'd do what she could to make things right, but she wouldn't give him a chance to steal her heart. It was too risky. She wasn't sure she could take another blow like that.

"You deserve love," Corrie said firmly. "If it's not Mack, well, that's okay. You'd know better than I would. I don't know him. But at some point you need to let *someone* in. You don't want to miss out on the perfect guy for you."

Darcy *did* know the perfect guy for her. But thanks to their past and her choices, they were stuck apart. Mack had kissed her, but how did she know that wasn't based on the old Darcy? The one he'd married? The one he'd made—and lost—a baby with. The one he'd let go.

He didn't know her now. That mattered. And in the three weeks she had left on the farm, there was no real way to get to know him again.

Mack had tried to figure out a way to frame the request. In seven years, he'd never asked about the Christmas ornaments he and Darcy had had on their first—and only—tree together. He wasn't going to go in his mother's house without her knowledge, and he for damn sure wasn't going to ask Chase.

So it looked as though he had to suck it up and face his demons and his mother's questions.

He stopped in on his lunch, which was what he framed the time between leaving his vet practice and getting out to the farm. Mom was there, of course, and she brightened right up when she saw him.

"Mack." She stepped out of the doorway and gestured him in. Little flurries of snow accompanied him and she shut the door quickly. "What's going on? We don't usually see you in the middle of the day."

He dropped a kiss on his mother's head. "Hi, Mom." He raised his voice so his father could hear him over the TV in the den. "Hey, Dad."

His father's reply carried over the noise of the television. Mom rolled her eyes. "This one's about how Sumatrans made their pottery." Mack had to grin despite the nerves in his belly. Dad loved history programs. In the winter, the off-season, he had them on almost nonstop and was enthralled by all of it. Mack had asked once why they just didn't go visit the places he was so interested in, and Dad had just looked at him and said, "I'm an armchair traveler."

Fair enough.

Mom led him into the kitchen, where she had something in the oven that smelled fantastic. "Lasagna," she said with a faint smile as she caught him sniffing the air the way a hound might scent a bird. "There will be extra for you."

"Do you take extras to Chase?" He knew the answer but was trying to stall on his actual request.

"Sometimes. But that boy can cook. He even likes it." She gave him an amused look, then got out a mug. "Coffee?"

"Sure," he murmured, taking in the scene as she poured the mug from the pot that always seemed to be at the ready. He'd always pictured himself in the same kind of marriage his parents had. In terms of the affection, the love, the way they still enjoyed each other's company. He'd thought he'd found that in Darcy. But he'd been wrong.

He accepted the mug she held out. She'd let him sit and stew as long as he needed to spit out what he needed to say. It was a time-honed technique that had worked way too well when he was a kid.

Still worked now as an adult.

They made small talk for a few minutes when he finally blurted out, "I need the Christmas stuff Darcy and I had."

She set her mug on the table and leveled a serious gaze on him. "What are you going to do with it?"

"Put it on a tree," he said, and she nodded, pushed back from the table and started toward the back bedroom. He rose and followed her.

"Do you know what you're doing, Mack?" she asked as she flicked on the light and gestured to the two cardboard boxes sitting on the floor by the bed. Not in the attic? *Mack and Darcy, Christmas* was written in his mother's neat hand in black marker on the lids of both.

I don't have a clue, he wanted to say. *No. Freaking. Clue.* But instead he asked, staring at the boxes, "How did you know?"

She gave him a tiny smile. "Helen's daughter saw you

driving home last night with a big old tree in the bed of your truck. Helen called me as soon as she heard."

Mack opened his mouth, then snapped it shut. There wasn't much to say to that. He should have known his mother would hear about it from one of her friends. Her social network was impressive. He shook his head. "I see. Well. Thanks."

She shrugged. "I hope you know what you're doing, Mack. Not only for your sake, but for hers. Darcy is so fragile."

He almost laughed as he lifted one of the boxes. Darcy was anything but fragile. She was tough, far tougher than she probably knew. "I'll be careful."

She picked up the other box and followed him down the hall lined with family pictures. He was careful not to knock any off with the big box. He put the first one in the truck and came back for the second.

"See that you are," she said quietly, and he didn't even pretend to misunderstand what she meant.

Mack wasn't sure what to do with the boxes, so he put them in his own spare bedroom—not the one he used as a weight room, but the back one he almost never went in. The one that would have been the baby's room. The one that, in the back of the closet, still had a crib in its box. It also had a box of stuff Darcy had left when she split. He wasn't sure why he kept any of it. After several months of no contact, he'd realized she wasn't coming back.

He didn't open the closet.

Apparently, he could have saved himself the trouble of quasi hiding the tree on the back deck and just left it on the front porch. He should have known someone would see and report it to his mother.

He propped his hands on his hips and surveyed the tree. It wasn't bad, considering they'd chopped it down in the dark. There was a fairly sizable hole on one side, but if he angled the tree a little to the left, it was facing the wall.

Better.

He peeled off his gloves and dropped them on the coffee table. Trees like that tore you to pieces if you weren't careful. He poured water in the stand and left the house for the tree farm.

Darcy had spent the better part of the day throwing herself into her work, making wreaths with the team and filling orders. It kept thoughts of Mack at bay. Thoughts of how she had to finish what she'd started with her impulsive Christmas-tree idea.

She mentally kicked herself for the zillionth time. It had been a stupid idea, an uncharacteristically impulsive thing that she never did anymore. Impulsiveness led to mistakes. Mistakes couldn't be undone. She was very careful not to make them, much less ones like this.

She wired the spruce boughs into the large wreath she was making for the wall of the Methodist church. This one would be three feet across, but fairly simple. It would have a huge red bow that'd she make next. It was a good way to stay occupied.

Until her thoughts slipped back to Mack's mouth on hers.

She stabbed herself with the wire and it went through her glove. She pulled the glove off with a muttered curse and Wendy, one of the longtime employees, sent her an amused look.

"Mack on the brain?"

Darcy shut her eyes and then opened them to examine her finger. "No more than usual," she muttered, which could have meant anything.

"He's quite a catch," Wendy said, all seriousness now.

Darcy felt her back go up. "Of course he is."

"But so are you," she said quietly. Darcy could only blink at her as she went on, "I don't know what went wrong, but he sure looks at you like you matter to him."

Like you matter to him. Those words echoed in her brain as they got through the evening, as she sold trees and decorations and poured hot chocolate and made sure the Christmas station was playing at the proper volume.

He hadn't said anything to her about the tree. She had a trunkful of lights at the ready, thinking he might need them. Since it'd been her idea and all and she'd practically forced him to get the tree.

He looked up then, across the cold barn, and his gaze locked right on hers. As if he'd known she was looking at him. The corner of his mouth quirked up in an almost smile. Then someone said something to him and he turned around and disappeared from her vision.

They closed the place down at seven. It didn't take long. Darcy locked the money in the safe and waved to the departing workers.

Except Mack, of course. He was at his truck. Waiting for her.

"So," he said as she approached. "I've got this tree. It needs some love." He arched an eyebrow at her and she suppressed a smile.

"Does it, now?" she said. "I need to eat first and give Uncle Joe a report. I can be at your place in—" she looked at her phone "—less than an hour."

"Sounds good," he said.

She didn't watch him leave. She walked back to the house and it took more willpower than it should have to not look back.

She was at his house, as she'd said, in less than an hour. As she did every night now, she'd delivered her report, her handwritten notes, all the receipts to Uncle Joe so he could pore over them. It made him happy and helped him feel as though he was still a part of everything. She ate a quick dinner, showered and changed, then drove into town.

She pulled the bags with the lights out of her trunk. Their first tree had had multicolor lights on it. She'd bought the same for him.

He opened the door almost as soon as she knocked. "Hey," he said, stepping out of the way.

"Hey," she echoed, surprised to realize she was a little shy. She brushed past him, smelling his soap or shampoo. He smelled yummy enough to make the heat begin to rise in her, just a little.

Even a little was too much.

She gave him her coat when he reached for it and toed off her boots. She saw bags on the coffee table, too. He'd been shopping. Or maybe his mom had.

She mentally winced. What did Mack's mom think of Darcy now? Of her being back in town and even remotely in Mack's life? His mom hadn't been thrilled with the marriage—that had been clear from the start.

It didn't matter. Darcy wasn't staying.

She pushed aside the thoughts and stepped into the living room. He'd lit a fire, she noted. She looked at the tree and then at him, a small smile tugging at her mouth.

"Not too bad for being dark," she said cheerfully, walking over to inspect it. "And you didn't—" She turned around and found him right behind her.

"Didn't what?" His voice was low.

"Trust me," she whispered, and almost closed her eyes, the fragrant tree at her back, the man at her front.

But he stepped back and the moment shattered at her feet like a glass ornament handled carelessly. She swallowed hard and turned back toward the tree.

"It's got a big hole," he said, and his voice was a little rough. So she hadn't imagined the charged moment they'd just shared. "But not too bad for being in the dark."

She smiled and fingered the tip of a branch. If you smoothed the needles right on a spruce tree, they wouldn't draw blood. "I brought lights."

"I got some ornaments." He paused for a moment, a faraway expression on his face. "Nothing fancy."

She shrugged. "It's your tree, Mack."

Not theirs. *His.* Her observation wasn't lost on her, and she tried to ignore the little stab of pain it brought.

He didn't correct her and she started unloading the boxes of lights while he put on the leather gloves and started winding them, tucking them in the branches. The radio played softly in the background from somewhere—the kitchen, maybe—and she found it soothing to work with him like this, companionable. The past seemed to have receded somewhat as she realized she liked Mack. Not as the man she remembered, but as the man he was now.

That was every bit as dangerous as the memories.

She handed him the last string and he hooked it up, then wrapped it around the tree. He stepped back and she leaned over to click off the light on the end table. He peeled the gloves off and nodded as they both took it in. Transformed, it glowed bight and Darcy sighed. "It's beautiful. You did a good job."

"Thanks." He tossed the gloves on the floor and reached for a bag. "Let's see what we've got here."

He'd bought a mishmash of brightly colored ornaments. Nothing real personal. She didn't ask where their stuff was. She wasn't sure she could handle seeing it, even after all this time.

"Plastic," he explained as the smaller dog—Lilly—demonstrated the reason why glass would have been bad. Her tail slapped several on the floor and as they rolled away a calico cat leaped out from under a chair to chase them.

Darcy had to laugh. "Maybe they should go up. Out of tail range," she added doubtfully. "I've seen parents with little kids do that."

Then she froze at her own stupid, thoughtless words. The past came roaring back and sat right down in the living room with them, making itself comfortable in the sharpness of the silence. She opened her mouth again, but for the life of her couldn't think of anything to say that would make it better, so she clamped it shut again.

"Yes," he agreed quietly, and she heard the threads of pain in his tone, even in that one word. "They do. So should pet owners." When she turned to look at him—

Is he really going to let me off that easy?—he gave her a small smile.

He was.

"Want something to drink?" he asked, heading for the kitchen. "I've got beer. No wine, I'm afraid," he said, "but there's some diet Mountain Dew in here, too."

She should go. Before all this became too much and something happened. Something that even now she could feel tugging at her. "Beer's fine."

He held up two different kinds, and she pointed at her choice. He poured them each a glass and handed her one before going back in the living room. Which was far too cozy with the fire crackling, and the lights from the tree sending out a soft light. The dogs were asleep on the hearth, and a wave of longing hit her hard. This was all she'd ever wanted. And someday he'd share it with someone else. She took a drink of her beer and sat down on the couch. He did, too, and she sent him a sideways look as he turned on the TV.

What she should do was go home. There was no reason not to. The night was clear as a bell, if cold. No snow, no ice, no excuses to stay.

He put on a movie, a recent action flick. "Did you see this one?"

She shook her head. She hadn't been to see a movie in ages. "Nope. Missed it."

"Me, too. We can watch it while we decorate."

He got up and went to make popcorn and she tried really hard to make herself leave. Listing all the reasons this was a bad idea. Why it was always a bad idea to get attached.

But when he came back, set the bowl on the table and handed her a paper towel for her fingers, she knew she wasn't fooling even herself anymore. They shared the bowl, sipped beer, hung ornaments and laughed at the antics on-screen.

And Darcy found herself tipping toward him a little more.

Chapter Eleven

This was how it'd always been with them, and there was a time Mack would have given anything for one more night like this.

Be careful what you wish for. He could hear his mother's voice in his head, same as when he was a kid. There was always a price. No doubt. But Darcy was here now, her fingers bumping his in the popcorn bowl, her knee touching his thigh when she tucked her feet under her on the couch after they'd finished the tree. He didn't look at her, or pull away, and neither did she.

Finally, he'd had as much as he could take. The next time their fingers brushed, he twined hers in his. Her head snapped around, her eyes wide and luminous in the soft light of the tree and the TV. He pulled her in and kissed her. Her mouth was a little slick from the butter. He tasted the beer, the saltiness of the popcorn and the sweetness of the butter. She opened to him right away, as though maybe she'd been waiting for this, too.

It felt like a first kiss.

He sank deeper and pulled her in. She turned her body so she folded right into him, her arms around his neck. When he lowered her to the couch, his mouth still on hers, she didn't protest.

He pressed a kiss into her neck, feeling the flutter of her pulse there. It kept pace with his own. She ran her hands down his back and turned her face back to his when he slid a hand under her sweater. Her skin was so soft, so smooth, and he felt her inhale sharply at his touch. He lifted his head and looked her in the eye, seeing the desire and heat there, and the uncertainty, too. "You okay?" he asked, his voice a rasp in his throat. He didn't bother to shift away from her, so he knew she felt the hard length of him pressed into her thigh. Her eyes were molten, and he held still, wanting this so badly.

She lifted up and nipped his bottom lip, but he didn't lower back down. "Darce. I need to hear you say it." He was about to lose his mind, but he'd walk away if he had to, if it was what she needed.

"Yes," she whispered, and there was a small wobble in her voice. She lifted her eyes and met his and he saw the uncertainty was gone. "Yes," she repeated. "I'm okay, Mack." Then she smiled that smile, the one that always made his blood go hot, and he dropped his forehead to hers, relief flooding him, along with something much hotter, and much more intense.

Since he knew where this was heading, he stood up and held out a hand. They'd be better off in his bed than on this slippery leather couch. She took it and walked with him the short steps to his room. There was a slight tremor in her fingers, and when he drew her over to the bed, she laid a hand on his chest. In the faint moonlight that came through the window, he saw the intensity on her face. "What is it, Darce?"

She pleated his shirt in her fingers, then looked back up. "It's been a long time for me, Mack."

"Yeah?" He tugged her sweater up and she lifted her arms for him to slide it off. Her skin was creamy in the pale light. "Me, too, honey."

She seemed to relax then, and reached for the hem of his shirt, which he stripped off and tossed, then pulled her in, feeling the heat of her skin and the raspy lace of her bra on his skin. He closed his eyes, buried his face in her hair and groaned. "Darcy." There were no more words, and yet too many to say. She ran her hands up his arms to his face, which she pulled down to hers, and kissed him. Heat, passion, sweetness, all in one kiss.

He was a goner.

He reached behind her and unhooked the bra, which she shrugged off her shoulders and let it fall. She let out a laughing little "Eep!" when he bent and took those rosy, luscious nipples in his mouth. They were already peaked for him and he played with them both, with his tongue and his fingers, until she was gasping.

He kissed her throat, that sweet little pulse jumping even more now, and reached for the snap of her jeans as she reached for his. It took a little fumbling to get things down—her leg got stuck and she was hopping around trying to kick her pants off until he finally grabbed it and yanked and she went back on the bed with a giggle and a bounce of those glorious breasts. He landed beside her, his own grin so wide he was pretty sure his face was going to split in two. No matter. He'd be a damn happy man.

"Hey," she said softly, and he traced a line with one finger down her chest—a slight detour each way for her nipples—over her smooth belly and the scar there. He stopped there, running his fingers over the roughness of the scar. She reached for his hand and he shook his head.

"Mack—don't—"

"It's part of you, Darcy." It was part of him, too, but he didn't say that. He did lean down and kiss it before slipping farther to the curls at the juncture of her thighs, into the damp heat he found there. She gave a little gasp and he shifted his body. "While I'm here…"

Her legs fell open and he settled in. She grasped his head as he rolled his tongue and fingers around in the sweetness that had always been Darcy.

Darcy was losing her mind. Oh, Mack had always been good at this, so good, so very good. She bucked and he threaded his arms through her legs, resting his hands on her belly, a gentle pressure to hold her in place as he worked his magic. The pressure built like a wave and crashed over her just as fast as she gasped his name. Then his big body was covering hers as he held her through the tremors. She heard the crinkle of the condom package and he was inside her. A shudder racked his body as he held himself still, and pushed up on his forearms.

"Darcy—I'm not going to last long—" he gritted out, and she smiled and started moving against him. Turnabout was fair play and if he was going to make her lose her mind, well, she was going to return the favor.

The joke was on her. She matched him stroke for stroke and held on as he loved her, as the sweet pressure built, and he threw his head back as his whole body strained and shuddered. She followed him right over, the shock and pleasure of the second orgasm floating her gently to the ground.

He lay on her for a minute, breathing hard. "Wow."

She laughed and ran her hands up his sweaty back. "Yeah. Wow." But under all the sweetness was a bit of panic. Nothing had changed. Or rather, it'd gotten better, and it had been fantastic all those years ago. If it had been because they were so in love the first time around, what did that mean now?

She pushed the thoughts away. This might be her only chance to be like this with Mack, when she'd thought it was over for good. This was a gift, even if she'd pay for it later.

He rolled off her, onto his back, and his fingers found hers. They lay in the dark, and Darcy felt the dampness of tears leaking from her eyes.

"Stay," he said quietly, and she wasn't sure if he meant forever, or just tonight.

She wanted to, but her aunt and uncle— "I'm not sure, Mack."

He turned his head to look at her, then shifted and ran his thumb over the moisture at her eyes. "Please." Then, in a lighter tone, he added, "We never actually made it into the bed. We're on the covers." In the dark she saw his grin, and she was lost.

She sat up and scooted back toward the pillows, peeling the covers back, a wicked smile on her gorgeous face. "Well. Can't have that, can we?"

He followed her.

Darcy cracked one eye the next morning. The sky was barely light and Mack was still sleeping, one arm thrown over her like the way he used to sleep. The way they'd slipped into this so easily scared her. She knew why it could never be casual with them, and it made her heart hurt. He didn't stir as she slipped out from under his arm and tiptoed around and gathered up her clothes. She dressed quickly and quietly and let herself out into the cold predawn stillness. She shivered the whole drive home, not so much from the freezing temps but from the loss of the heat she'd shared with Mack. He wouldn't be happy she'd left. But she knew it was for the best. They'd crossed too many lines, and while she couldn't undo that, she could try to draw new ones.

She parked at the house and saw the kitchen light was on. Left on? Or was Marla up?

Darcy rested her head on the steering wheel. She was an adult. No one was going to say anything to her.

She let herself in the side door and saw that it had been left on. It wasn't quite time for Marla to be up yet. Darcy crawled back under the cold blankets of her childhood bed and stared at the ceiling, trying not to relive the night before and finding it impossible.

Marla gave her a knowing smile when she walked in the kitchen a couple of hours later. "So. Did you and Mack have a nice time?"

Darcy's face heated in spite of herself. "Yes. The tree looks nice."

"Mmm-hmm. Took all night to decorate, huh?" There was no censorship in her tone, but Darcy felt slapped down anyway.

"Something like that," she murmured, and grabbed a mug. Thank God there was coffee. She'd had very little sleep, thanks to what had turned out to be a very active night. As if they'd been making up for lost time. But Darcy knew better. There was no way to make it up, to recover what they'd lost. Or to start over and make something new.

Marla laid her hand on Darcy's arm. "Darcy. Be careful. If you're going to leave again, don't set yourself up for heartbreak."

She gave Marla a smile that was more a curving of her lips than a real smile. "I know. I'll be careful. I don't want to go through that again." That was God's honest truth.

As her aunt walked away, Darcy tried to ignore the little voice that told her it was already too late, that she was going to hurt like crazy when she left. That all her hard work, all her careful defenses had been for nothing when the man could strip her bare with just a look. She'd destroyed the last of them herself when she'd fallen apart in his arms last night.

Seemed she'd never learn.

Despite Darcy's predawn exit, Mack was in a good mood the next morning. Oh, he knew this didn't really change anything—no way it really could—but damn. Having her in his bed again was like an early Christmas gift to himself. To both of them.

He hoped this maybe meant they could put the past behind them, where it belonged.

He came into work, actually whistling, and Jennifer narrowed her eyes at him. "You got some, didn't you?"

He did a double take. "What?"

She sighed. "I recognize the signs. The loose walk. The perma-grin. You're whistling, for Pete's sake. Yeah. I'm hoping it was Darcy, otherwise you're a fool."

"Ah." He took a moment to think it through.

"I won't say anything," she added. "You know that. But, Mack... Is it a good idea?"

He rubbed his hand between his eyes. "Doesn't matter now, does it, Jenn?"

She shook her head. "Sure it does. She's leaving. You're taking away her reason to stay."

I should be her reason to stay. But he didn't say that. "What reason is that?"

Jenn looked at him as if he were nuts. "Her farm, dimwit. Why should she stay? Why will she ever come back? You guys are turning it into a subdivision and her family's moving to Arizona. If you think you're going to win her back this way, you're going about it all wrong."

Mack's head spun. "She didn't want the farm."

Jenn smacked his arm. Hard. "You're an idiot, Mack. Really. I expected better from you. You figure it out. I can't tell you what to do. I don't know Darcy. But I do know that if a man wanted me as bad as you want her, he'd damn well better put forth some effort to make me stay."

She was right. Of course she was right.

He was an idiot. And he'd overlooked one very important detail. He wasn't going to get her to stay *for him*. She needed a reason to leave Chicago, something that mattered to her. And Jenn was right—he and Chase were destroying the one place she loved more than anything.

"I don't have a lot of time," he said more to himself than to her. And really, did he want her to stay? Did he want her to be part of his life? Was he ready to go there again?

He wasn't sure.

Jenn had moved on to the end of the row, and the cacophony of hungry dogs and cats allowed him the lux-

ury of no conversation. His thoughts bounced back and
forth between his night with Darcy and Jenn's words.

When Mack arrived at the farm, Darcy had hoped
that she'd be out on the back forty somewhere, but of
course that wasn't the case. He walked right up to her,
in front of all the other people that were milling around,
and said, very quietly, "Hi."

"Hi," she said back, more of a breath than a vocal-
ization.

There was an awkward moment while they looked
at each other, then away. *Crap.* She felt her face burn.

"You okay?"

She looked at him almost shyly. "Yeah."

Then he stepped back and gave her a little smile
before heading around back. Darcy took a breath and
the cold air burned her lungs. Well. Anyone watching
knew exactly what had happened with them. Wonderful. She took a quick look around, but it was hard to
tell with so many people moving around who had noticed and who hadn't.

She threw herself into the work, trying not to cue
in to him in the most primal way possible. He seemed
to be everywhere she was. Or maybe she was just hy-
peraware of him.

That was probably it.

She smiled at the couple in front of her, and it took
her a minute to realize the woman was looking at her
with a bemused smile.

Recognition clicked in. "Oh, my gosh. Cheryl?"

The other woman smiled. "I didn't think you recognized me." She laughed.

"No, I—I was distracted, I guess," she admitted, and

came around the table to hug her former friend, whom she hadn't seen in ages. Since before she'd left for good.

"I bet I know why," Cheryl said with a low laugh. "I see Mack here."

"Ah." She darted a quick glance in the direction he'd been, and saw he had his head bent in conversation with a gorgeous black-haired woman. She tore her eyes away and ignored the sharp stab of jealousy. "Yes, well, he's been helping Uncle Joe."

Cheryl raised an eyebrow but didn't say anything else. She gestured to a tall man who was holding a little girl on his hip. She couldn't be more than three, as blond as her mother, wearing an adorable red velvet beret. Darcy couldn't stop her smile.

"Oh, Cheryl. She's gorgeous. She looks just like you!"

"Thanks, Darce. This is my husband, Jake, and daughter, Olivia. We met at college. Been married five years."

Yes, Darcy knew that. Marla had told her, had sent the invite on, and of course Darcy had sent her regrets. "I remember."

Cheryl let it go. "Can I have your number? I'd love to get together for coffee if you've got time."

Darcy's first instinct was to say no, as much as she wanted to reconnect with her old friend. All these connections were like a vine, binding her to this place, holding her back when she knew she had to leave. But at the same time— She pulled out her phone. "Sure. I'd like that."

Mack caught her eye over Cheryl's head as Darcy slid her phone back in her pocket. He'd seen. He'd know what it cost her to connect. He gave her a private little smile and her heart flipped.

She got through the rest of the day and headed up to the house after. It was cold, colder than it'd been yet.

It made the air dry, and the snow was squeaky under her boots. She'd managed to avoid Mack, but she was pretty sure it wouldn't last for long.

He could be determined.

She went in the kitchen and peeled off her layers. She usually just wore a thermal undershirt, a fleece jacket and a vest. Today it'd been cold enough for the full-on parka, even in the shelter of the barn. She unlaced her boots and left them at the door, and peeled out of her wool socks. She had cotton ones on under them, and long underwear under her jeans.

In the kitchen, her aunt and uncle smiled at her, and she pushed down thoughts of Mack and all the stupid feelings he invoked in her.

"Pretty cold," Joe commented, and she plopped into the seat opposite him, handing the papers to him over the cracked and worn linoleum table.

"Yes, but it didn't keep people away," she said simply. "They're just more likely to choose a precut tree rather than go tromping around in the woods."

He grunted. "Mack had extra cut?"

"Of course," she said, getting up to pour a cup of coffee. Decaf, of course, but it smelled good enough she didn't care.

Another grunt, this one of approval. "Smart boy, that one."

In some things, maybe. But Darcy wasn't going to go there. "You trained him, Uncle Joe."

Her uncle laughed, and she smiled back. He was looking better. His color was better, and while still he tired easily, he was coming back pretty good. Marla set a steaming plate in front of her. Chicken, sure, but also mashed potatoes and gravy. Her mouth watered.

Darcy knew if she kept eating like this, she'd need a whole new wardrobe come the first of the year, but she couldn't bring herself to care when she was this hungry.

"How is Mack?" Marla's question was conversational, but Darcy sensed the potential minefield.

"Fine," she said as she dredged a bite of chicken through the potatoes and gravy. "This is excellent, Aunt Marla." She popped the bite in her mouth, hoping her dodge worked.

"Thank you, dear," Marla said. Joe had retired to the living room and his favorite chair and was poring over the records. It appeared he'd pulled out last year's, as well. He was oblivious to the twist in conversation. Marla folded her arms on the table and leaned forward earnestly. "I have to ask. Are you and Mack considering reconciliation?"

Darcy opened her mouth, then shut it again. She pushed a few peas out of the gravy river on her plate. "No. I don't believe we are, Aunt Marla." The words were surprisingly hard to say. Because she wanted it to be true? Or because it hadn't occurred to her?

Who was she kidding? Of course it had occurred to her. How could it not?

Marla sat back. "I will say that's too bad. He's a great guy and you deserve the happiness you had with him."

Darcy shoved her plate away, all appetite gone. No, she didn't. She'd tossed it away as if it didn't matter. Made no difference at this point if it was true or not—he believed it was. "It's a little more complicated than that, Aunt Marla. You, of all people—you know that." She'd been the one to pick up the pieces. Or as many pieces as Darcy had allowed.

Compassion softened her aunt's features. "I do know

that, honey. I know that very well. But a lot of things brought you back here. If there's a chance, an opportunity, why not take it?"

It wasn't too far from what Darcy had been thinking, yet worlds away. She hadn't been thinking in terms of reconciliation. She'd been thinking of apologizing, maybe getting him to understand where she'd been coming from. Somewhere along the line that had changed. And she hadn't even realized it until now.

"Too much time has gone by," she said simply. "We're different people now. That's not a bad thing."

Marla shook her head. "No, it's not, that's true. But you've locked yourself down so tight, you won't let anyone in. How is that a good thing? You're so young."

Darcy gave a little shrug, as she had done when she was a teenager and pinned in the corner by her aunt. She didn't like being cornered. But she wasn't going to explain herself. She didn't think she'd shut herself down that tightly. She was practical, sure, but that wasn't a bad thing. It'd gotten her this far in life.

In her bed that night, she listened to the wind howl. It battered snow against the window—in this kind of temperature, it was little more than hard kernels of snow—and just seemed to underscore her loneliness. She was under the quilt in her old bedroom in her childhood home, instead of in the bed of the man who'd loved her. Who'd married her and done right by her when she got pregnant.

And she'd left him.

She curled onto her side and slipped into dreams of what could have been.

Chapter Twelve

The next couple of days were busy. She and Mack had fallen into a kind of truce. She didn't know what he wanted, but he wasn't pushing her. He was friendly, sometimes flirty, and every time he gave her that slow smile, her insides turned into a total puddle. Was he waiting for her to come to him? That didn't seem likely. Mack wasn't a game player. He was straightforward and solid. But he was clearly holding back. Waiting for her to make the next move?

Racking her brain meant she wasn't paying attention. And not paying attention meant she was recruited to go with Mack out to the far field to check one of the warming stations.

"I can just go," she offered, and saw him cock his eyebrow. "I mean, I'm sure you've got other things to do."

"Let's go," he said, and walked to the ATV. She trot-

ted behind, mentally kicking herself for thinking she
could get away from him.

They got in, and while she was grateful for the roar
of the engine, she was pressed right up against him in
the little vehicle. This was really a one-person ride, not
for two, especially when the past of those two people
crowded in and seemed to both shove them apart while
cementing them together.

She tucked her face in the neck of her zipped-up
parka, trying to protect against the stinging wind.

At the station he cut the engine and got out almost
before it came to a stop. She hopped after him, feeling
resentful and angry and knowing it wasn't his fault.

No, she wanted more and was angry with herself
for wanting it.

She restocked while he checked the errant coffeemaker. She loved that he was so handy, had always been,
and that didn't appear to have changed at all.

By the time he'd finished she was done. "Why am
I here?"

"That's a good question," he said mildly, and all it
did was make her madder.

"Mack. You didn't need me out here. And you won't
talk to me—"

He was in front of her in about two strides. She
gasped and backed up, but the wall was behind her
and he'd planted both arms on either side of her, cag-
ing her in but not actually touching her. The look in his
eyes was molten and she swallowed hard. He didn't say
a word, just kept his eyes on hers until the last moment
when his mouth came down on hers. Hard. There was
no mercy in his kiss. He didn't touch her, but she felt
the tension and hardness of his body even without the

contact. She fisted her hands at her sides and kissed him back, giving as good as she got. Then she stopped thinking altogether.

He pulled away and the only sound other than the blood roaring in her ears was the rasp of their breathing in the quiet of the cabin. She lifted her fingers to touch her mouth, realized they were shaking and dropped her hand again.

"Damn it, Darcy," he said, but there wasn't any heat in the words. "You've got it all wrong." He stepped back, his eyes still on hers, and she could barely breathe. "All wrong," he repeated, and turned away.

She moved quickly and grabbed his arm. "What? What do I have wrong, Mack?" If he could tell her, if she could know, it would make all this so much easier.

He shook his head. "I just wanted to love you. But you wouldn't let me, then or now. Why is that?"

She stared up at him. It had never been that easy. "Because that's not how it worked for us. And, Mack, come on. We have too much baggage to make anything work. It's better left behind."

"Not a day goes by, Darcy, that I don't think of you. Of the baby. That I don't wonder what if. If we'd stayed together, would we have more? What would they look like?" His voice was so raw tears burned in her eyes and she knew what she had to do.

"I can answer part of that. No. There wouldn't be any more." Her voice was shaky and the words almost stuck in her throat. But it had to be said and it had to be said now.

"Because you didn't want them?" There was bitterness in his tone, and it made her heart ache even more that he'd think that of her, even if it was in anger.

She took a deep breath and looked him in the eye. "No. Because I can't have any more. I can't get pregnant, Mack."

Mack's ears were ringing. Darcy stood in front of him. Her mouth was still forming words, but he wasn't hearing any of them. *Can't get pregnant.* "What do you mean, you can't get pregnant?"

She lifted her chin. "From the damage of the miscarriage and the accident, the odds of me ever conceiving again are nearly zero. I'm more likely to be struck by lightning." Her tone was nearly expressionless.

Shock was reverberating around in him, making her words bounce around in his brain like a bunch of loose Ping-Pong balls. He moved away from her and she stayed where she was.

"Mack. I'm so sorry." Now there was pain in her words, regret and sorrow. She'd known this for how long?

"How long?" The words ripped from his throat. "How long have you known?"

Her eyes widened, but she said nothing. And he knew.

"You've known since you left," he said, almost wonderingly. "And you never said one word. Not one." And hell if he'd ever thought to ask her. He'd said, over and over, they could have another baby. How much he wanted to have a baby with her.

And she'd said nothing. Why not? If she hadn't been able to tell him, why hadn't the doctors told him?

She looked away and he saw her visibly fighting for control of her emotions. Then she looked back at him. "Yes. I knew the possibility was there. And it was confirmed later."

"After you'd already left."

"Mack, the doctor said there was a chance I couldn't get pregnant again! Remember? But you were so dead set on having another one, when I wasn't even out of the hospital yet."

She was already moving toward the door. "I'm walking back up. There's nothing more to say about this. I'm sorry. I really am. But I didn't see any reason to tell you when it was clearly over with us."

It wasn't until she'd left and the swirl of snow she'd let in on her exit had settled that he realized what she'd said.

It'd been a long time since Mack drank enough to, well, get drunk. And he was only half surprised when Chase showed up on his doorstep, grim-faced and tense.

Mack let his brother in and went back and collapsed on the couch. He could still feel, damn it. There wasn't enough alcohol in the world to fill the hole Darcy's words had made in his heart.

"Why are you here?" Or at least that was what he meant to say. It seemed to come out a little slurred.

"Darcy called me. Told me I should check on you." Even in his state, Mack could hear the bitterness in his brother's voice. "What the hell did she do to you?"

He let his head loll back on the couch. Closing his eyes was bad. Things started to spin. Maybe he'd had a little more than he thought. "Nothing."

The crash and clink of glass pierced his mental fog. "All these say otherwise," Chase said as he left the room, the bottles clinking in his hands. "Tell me," he said quietly when he came back in. "It must have been bad if she called me."

Something seemed off about that, but Mack wasn't

quite tracking well enough to get it. Wait. There it was. "Darcy called *you*?" Wow. Cold day in hell, and all that.

"Yeah," he said. "She asked me to check on you. Why?"

"She told me she can't have any more babies," he blurted, then winced. Even in this condition, he didn't want to talk about it. It wasn't Chase's business. He wasn't sure it was even his own. Not anymore.

"Okay," Chase said, his voice level. "But you're not together."

Nope, he wasn't far enough gone to muffle the pain of those words. Damn it. "No."

Chase didn't say anything else. He got up, and when he came back he had a sandwich, which he handed to Mack. "You need this more than another beer."

Mack took it, but he wasn't so sure. What he really needed he was afraid he'd never have again.

His wife back.

The next morning Mack's head pounded. He'd earned the headache. He dragged himself through his day at his vet practice, and while he was perfectly pleasant to his staff, his patients and their owners, his office staff had clearly caught his underlying mood and were handling him with kid gloves.

He went out to the tree farm because it wasn't in his nature to shirk his duties just because it was awkward. He could handle it. Unless it came to his ex-wife, of course. It was becoming crystal clear he had no idea how to handle her.

He didn't see her when he first pulled in. Then he spotted her in her navy fleece jacket and red vest, a bright red hat covering her copper hair. He swallowed hard. She looked up then, spotted him and said something to Wendy, who laughed as she walked away.

Now she was walking toward him, her stride long and purposeful. He didn't move, just shoved his hands in his pockets and let her come, let her make the move. It wasn't in his court. This was all her.

"Can we talk?" Her brown eyes searched his and he saw the shadows on the fine skin under her eyes. She hadn't slept any better than he had.

He was tempted to say no way, but he didn't want to hurt her more. There'd been too much pain between them already. "Sure."

She turned and headed out the door, toward the house. He caught up with her and they walked, wordlessly, through the dark to the house.

Darcy was nervous. Her fingers shook as she unzipped her fleece jacket. She went into the kitchen. "Coffee?"

"Sure," he said, and his voice was quiet and cautious. She didn't blame him. She'd undone everything they'd rebuilt in the space of a few minutes last night. Again. Clearly, this was not meant to work out. Not ever.

She prepared the mugs and handed him one, unable to hide the fact her hands were shaking. The coffee sloshed in the mug but didn't spill. He took it with no comment other than a murmured "Thanks."

The best way out is through. She'd always loved the line from Whitman and it steadied her now. She sat and gestured for him to do the same.

"I'm sorry I sprang that on you like I did last night," she said. This needed to come from the heart, for her sake and his. "And I'm even more sorry I didn't tell you what the doctor said all those years ago."

Maybe it would have been easier for him if he'd known they could never be what he wanted so badly. Help him understand why she'd left. Tears burned her eyes. She'd thought she was done crying over this. But the magnitude of their loss hung between them now and she finally saw it differently. She'd held on to it as *hers* for so long she'd forgotten it was really *theirs*.

He sat back, his expression shuttered, his untouched coffee steaming on the table between them. She couldn't read him, wasn't sure what was going on in his head. "It was a lot to take in," she said quietly. "And I handled it all badly."

He rubbed his hand over his face. "Yeah, we both did." He sat forward, and rested his arms on the table, gaze on his fingers. She wanted to take his hand in hers, but instead threaded her fingers together tightly in her lap, so tightly it hurt. "Darce. I just wish you'd have told me. Let me carry some of it with you."

The dark thing, the deepest secret she held, battered against her chest. She wasn't going to tell him all of it. They had a chance to make a fragile peace. Telling him it had all been her fault wasn't going to help that, help him. And she owed him the chance to move on. So she said simply, "Me, too."

Because that was true. If she'd let him take some of it from her, would she have been able to stay? Hard to tell. She'd been a physical and emotional wreck at the time. She'd come back here, to the farm, to recuperate. He'd tried to get her to come home, but she'd refused. And he had eventually stopped arguing with her. Her physical injuries had healed, but her emotional ones ran much deeper. So deep, she didn't think she'd ever get around them. It was an ache she doubted would ever go away.

They sat for another few minutes and Darcy would have given almost anything to know what he was thinking. Then he said, "We need to get back."

Relieved it was over, she pushed back from the table and stood, reaching for his mug. But he caught her hand as he rose from his chair and tugged her around the table toward him. She stood in front of him, inhaling his scent, close but not close enough. She knew it'd never be close enough. Not now. He bent and pressed a soft kiss to her mouth. Then he dropped her hand and stepped back.

She put the mugs in the sink and they walked, wordless, back to the farm. The cheery, noisy bustle of happy families and Christmas music carried down the lane and for a minute Darcy felt suspended between two worlds—the one she had and the one she could have had if she'd stayed.

It was an eerie, unsettling feeling.

They managed to work around each other, but Darcy found the fragile peace they'd forged exhausting. She just wanted to curl up in bed and sleep. Until the day after Christmas, when she could finally go back to Chicago. *Home.*

Or was it?

She missed Chicago, but she'd begun to realize it wasn't quite home. Not the way this place was. Was that because she'd grown up here? Or because she still had some kind of feelings for Mack?

It seemed best to just admit it. That there were clearly lingering feelings, but it was in no way enough to move forward on. If either of them had wanted to. And she did not. There was too much pain in the past that would bleed through to their present.

"It's not enough," she said out loud to the spruce tree in front of her. *There, I said it.* Now all she had to do was hang on to that for the rest of her stay and she could escape mostly unscathed.

Some things just couldn't be fixed, no matter how much you wished otherwise.

The next morning, Darcy disconnected her phone and set it on the table in Java, the coffee shop that had become her closest thing to a home office.

So far, things were moving fairly smoothly in Chicago. Mally had things well in hand, which didn't surprise Darcy. She opened her laptop to check for the file Mally had emailed during their conversation. Perusing her assistant's work, she realized that Mally didn't need Darcy's direction. She knew exactly what she was doing and was in fact fully qualified to take over Darcy's position if she wanted to step down.

She could step right in and Darcy could—what? Leave? And do what? Ross wouldn't give Mally Darcy's job, of course. Not right away. But Ross would move on, fill her position.

Darcy put the thoughts aside. No point in going there when it wasn't going to happen. She'd worked long and hard to get where she was and she wasn't going to throw it all over for—what? Definitely not for something she couldn't even define. That was reckless. And stupid. And so very un-Darcylike.

"Darcy. How are you?"

She looked up at the friendly voice to see Cheryl.

"Hi, Cheryl." She pulled her papers and laptop over so the other woman could sit if she wanted to.

Cheryl hesitated. "Are you sure? I don't want to bother you if you're working."

Darcy closed the laptop and gestured for her to sit down. "I'm completely sure. I could use a break anyway. I'm sorry we haven't been able to get together yet. How are you?"

Cheryl smiled. "Good. Busy. Decided to treat myself to a latte today since we got word that we're being considered as adoptive parents for a teenage mother's baby."

Darcy's heart stuttered. "Wow, Cheryl, that's wonderful. When will you know?"

"Soon. She's about seven months along. She's a good girl, got in a tough situation and wants to give her baby the best life she can. It's not a done deal, but I hope…" She trailed off and took a sip of the latte.

Darcy reached over and touched her hand. "I hope so, too, Cheryl."

"There's something I've been wondering," Cheryl said quietly, her hands closed around her cup. She leveled her gaze at Darcy. "Why did you leave without saying goodbye? And why did you cut off all contact with me?"

Darcy sucked in a breath. There was pain in her old friend's voice, but no censure. She slid her laptop in her bag to give herself a second to regroup. Then she folded her arms on the table and looked right at Cheryl. "I'm not really sure. It hurt too much to be here, and everything was a reminder of what—of what I'd lost. I was just trying to move forward and I know I did a bad job of it." She'd rejected Cheryl's support, everyone's support. How stupid she'd been. "I was just so lost, I guess. In the grief. I'm so sorry I cut you off."

Cheryl nodded. "I figured that was what happened, but I needed to hear it for sure. I would have been there. I wanted to be there, Darce. A lot of people did."

So she was learning. All the bitterness she'd carried like a shield was withering away. She'd erected the shield as a defense to keep herself in, not to protect herself from people who cared. But that was exactly what had ended up happening.

"I wish you'd let me in," Cheryl said quietly now. "And I wish I'd tried harder to reach you. I didn't know what to do and I didn't try as hard as I could have."

Darcy's head came up sharply. "What? No, Cheryl, that's not what happened. You were there. That's all you needed to do, was to *be there*. And you were. I was the one who didn't know how to handle it. Or how to let anyone help me handle it. I just wanted it all to go away."

Cheryl cocked her head. "Did it?"

"No," Darcy admitted now. "Not really. I got good at kind of locking it away. Until I came back here."

A small smile ghosted across Cheryl's mouth. "I bet. There's something I need to tell you."

"What's that?"

"Olivia's middle name is Darcy."

Darcy's breath jammed in her throat. Cheryl couldn't have surprised her more if she'd hit Darcy with a hammer. "You—really? Oh," she said, and the word kind of fell from her lips. "Cheryl—"

"Yes, really." Cheryl's smile was looking decidedly damp around the edges, which was okay because Darcy knew hers was, too. "I just wanted you to know."

The lump in Darcy's throat was almost too big to breathe around. She reached for Cheryl's hand and held on tight, a connection she wished she'd accepted when it was offered all those years ago. "Thank you, Cheryl."

Chapter Thirteen

Mack showed up late at the tree farm. He looked a little ragged, and despite her best intentions to stay away,
she went up to him. He gave her a tired smile that didn't
reach his eyes. Concerned, she touched his arm. "Are
you okay?"

He rubbed his hand over his eyes. "Yeah. No. Rough
day."

Which told her nothing, since she could already see
that. "We can get by without you tonight if you need to
go home, Mack. Don't feel you need to stay."

He dropped his hand. "Thanks, but I need to stay."

Since he wasn't going to confide in her—why would
he?—she nodded. "Your call. Let me know if you
change your mind, though."

He said nothing as she walked away. Then—

"Darcy."

She stopped and turned. "Yes?"

He drew in a shaky breath. "It was an abuse case. Worst one I've seen yet. Dog beaten within an inch of his life and left out to die in the cold. He was frozen to the ground. I don't know if he'll survive, or if he'll ever be able to go to a new home." His voice was low, and the pain in his words fell heavily on her heart. Horror and anger fired there, too, that someone would treat an animal that way. Any living being.

She walked back toward him. "Oh, Mack. Do they know who did it?"

He shook his head. "No. Not yet. I hope they find the son of a bitch. Because it's more than the dog, Darce. What if this guy's doing this to his family? There's something wrong with a person who can hurt an animal this way."

She gave up and wrapped her arms around him, laid her head on his chest. His jacket was cold under her cheek. He wrapped his around her, too, and they stood there, by the side of his truck, Darcy feeling his warm breath on her hair. This was what they should have had. This was one of those moments that was out of time, from a life she didn't live but could have.

"He's got you," she said finally as she stepped back and looked up to meet his eyes. "And we'll hope the person who did this gets found soon."

"Thanks," he said quietly. "I see a lot in my job. A lot of broken animals, sick ones, too. But almost never something like this. I don't know how he survived as long as he did. I really don't. So I'll cut out early tonight, if it looks like things are under control, to go check on him. Jennifer's with him now."

"It's a Wednesday," Darcy said. "Our slowest day. It'll be fine, whenever you're ready to head out."

They walked to the barn in silence and he gave her hand a quick squeeze before heading the opposite way. Warmth fizzled through her, a little burst of surprise and happiness. He'd never touched her like that in public. She didn't know if anyone had seen.

She kept an eye on him through the evening, and he did leave early. That night, after she'd closed everything down and chatted with her aunt and uncle, she went up to her room and called Mack to check on the dog. She felt a little bit like a teenager as she lay flopped on her back across the bed, knees up. She almost wished for the days when there was a long phone cord to wrap around her finger.

"Hello?"

His voice was just as sexy over the phone as it was in person. Despite the reason for her call, her lady parts gave a little shimmy. She cleared her throat. "Hi. It's Darcy."

He gave what sounded like a pained chuckle. "I know. Everything okay out there?"

"Yeah. I just wanted to see how the dog is. If he's— well, if he's okay."

Mack sighed. "He's not okay, but he's holding. At this point, that's about all I can expect. Still touch-and-go. If he makes it through the night, his chances will be better."

"Poor guy," she said quietly.

"Yeah. I'm going to check him every hour until five, then I'll go home and catch a few hours of sleep while Jenn checks him."

"So you're staying at the clinic?" She knew Jennifer lived above the clinic. Maybe he stayed with her. And it was completely none of her business. Still, an odd twist slipped through her chest.

There was a rustling, as though he was moving around. "Yeah. I keep a cot here. I'll sleep in my office. Grabbed a pillow and blanket from home. I don't have to do it too often."

"That's good," she said.

There was a pause, but it wasn't uncomfortable. They were just quiet. Together.

"Darcy?"

"Yeah?" Why was she whispering?

"Thanks for calling."

"You're welcome."

She disconnected the call and stared up at the dark ceiling, feeling all kinds of fluttery and weird. Truth was, she could have waited until tomorrow to find out about the dog. She'd been concerned, yes, and saddened. But she'd wanted to check on Mack, too, and this had been a convenient excuse.

She rolled over and put the phone on the bedside table. She already missed his voice. Missed him. How sad was that?

"Two weeks until Christmas Eve," Joe announced at breakfast. "This upcoming Saturday will be almost as busy as the day after Thanksgiving. I'm going to meet with you and Mack to discuss a game plan."

Darcy spooned up more oatmeal. She had no idea what her aunt put in it, but it was good. It didn't matter if she didn't need the meeting. Uncle Joe did. "When?"

"Tonight. He'll come to the house when he gets here. We'll have it here, in the kitchen."

"I'll have pie," Marla broke in with a smile.

"Sounds good." If it hadn't been the last season, it would have been a different sort of meeting. Darcy wanted to ask why they'd never branched out into more sales, why they hadn't expanded the tours, why more promotion hadn't been done. Yes, some of that cost money, but they'd have earned it all back and then some. But she wasn't going to ask now. It was too late.

The farm had two weeks left. Then, after the new year, it'd be turned over to Mack and his brother to bulldoze. Appetite gone, she slid her chair back to carry her bowl to the sink. For all Mack still tugged at her heart, he was taking away the one thing that had always been a constant in her life. She needed to remember that.

"I'm so sad this place is closing," one woman said to Darcy later that evening after the meeting with Uncle Joe. "I've come out here since I was a little girl. Now I bring my kids. We look forward to it every year." The kids in question looked to be around five and nine, and happily sucking on the mini–candy canes Darcy had given them from her stash by the register.

"Me, too. We all are. But my aunt and uncle are going to retire. A tree farm is a lot of work." She'd said the same thing many times over the past couple weeks. But now she added, "It's been a wonderful experience, being a part of all these Christmases for all of these years."

The woman handed over the cash for the tree. "So much better than grabbing a tree at a big box store," she agreed. "I wish your aunt and uncle all the best in their retirement. Maybe they'll get lucky and find someone to take it over."

Darcy couldn't bring herself to say it'd been sold and would be parceled off into home lots. "Maybe," she said noncommittally, and smiled as she gave the woman her change.

As she watched them go, Wendy came up to her. "I heard her. Tough, isn't it?"

Darcy sighed. "She's not the only one. I've heard some variation of that several times each week. Some people aren't invested, you know? They'll just get a tree and move on. For others, it's a tradition. I never realized or appreciated how much that matters."

How shameful was that? She'd grown up in a business that catered to people's traditions and she'd still missed the point. Until now.

When it was too late.

Wendy nodded. "It is hard. I've made the same wreaths for a decade for the same people. I know who likes a little more spruce, and who to give the most juniper berries to. Who likes a bigger bow, who prefers flatter. I love to see their faces light up when they come pick them up. It's all part of the package of tradition. I'll miss it." She held out her hands and gave a little laugh. "I won't miss being stabbed fifty times a day by needles, though. Or getting pitch on my clothes."

Darcy smiled and shook her head ruefully. "No. I guess not."

Wendy went outside to check the wreaths and grave blankets—Darcy had sold a few—and it was quiet for a moment in the barn.

Until Mack walked in.

She'd asked him earlier about the dog, whom he'd named Fraser. He'd made it through the night. Mack was cautiously optimistic he'd pull through physically. Emotionally, he couldn't say.

She gave him a little smile. "Hey. Staying warm?"

He walked over and snitched a candy cane from her bowl. "Yep."

She frowned at him and teased, "Hey. Those are for paying customers only."

He arched an eyebrow and the look in his eyes went hot. Oh, my. An answering heat tugged low in her belly. "What's your price?"

Her mind went unhelpfully blank. "Um, well."

"How about I suggest one?" He moved behind the register and the plastic wrapper of the candy cane crinkled loudly as he put his hands on her shoulders. She licked her lips and could say nothing as he lowered his mouth to hers. "This okay?" he whispered, so close but still too far. In response, she pressed her mouth to his.

"Oops," Wendy's voice, and laughter, carried through the little cocoon that had woven around them. "Sorry to interrupt you kids."

He made a hungry sound in his throat and she pulled away, breathing hard, feeling her face flame. He pressed his lips to her forehead and gave a little chuckle.

"What's so funny?" she asked, not seeing anything humorous in the way her body revved and ached for his. For him. Plus, Wendy had caught them, even if she had stepped back out of the room.

"I don't know." He released her and stepped back. "We're just like a couple of teenagers sometimes."

She closed her eyes. "We're at work. This is a family place. When you and I kiss..." She trailed off.

There was a predatory light in his eyes now. "When you and I kiss, what?" he prompted.

She lifted her chin. "It gets out of control, okay? And this isn't the place for that." There. She'd said it.

He caught her chin. "You're right. It's not. Come to my place after we're done here."

He was completely serious. A thrill shivered down her spine. "I don't know."

He leaned down and gave her another quick kiss, and filched another candy cane. "The offer stands," he said, and sauntered out as another family made their way in. He sent her a wink over their heads and Darcy wasn't sure if she wanted to laugh or scream.

Or risk going over to his place. She knew exactly what was being offered there. But she wasn't sure she could spend the time with him and walk away whole when it was time for her to go.

Darcy went home afterward, gave her report to her uncle and headed upstairs to shower. As she stood under the steaming water, she wrestled with herself over Mack's invitation. It wasn't that she didn't want to go. She did. It was that she was afraid she was getting in too deep already.

Maybe it didn't even matter anymore. It was going to hurt when she left either way. This time, though, she could control it. And maybe minimize the regrets.

She turned off the water and toweled off quickly. In the steamy mirror she couldn't see the jagged scar on her abdomen, but she was aware it was there. Mack hadn't been put off by it. In her two sexual encounters in the seven years since her marriage ended, the room had been dark and it had been only one time. Each.

She dressed and dried her hair, combing it into place and securing it with a clip. A little mascara and she was good to go. She took a deep breath. From the time, she knew Uncle Joe and Aunt Marla would have retired to their room. She tossed a few necessities into a small bag she pulled from the closet and headed out before she lost her nerve.

Except Marla was in the kitchen.

Darcy froze, feeling for all the world like a teenager caught sneaking out when Marla's gaze fell to the bag, then up to Darcy's face. She surprised Darcy by laughing.

"Don't look so guilty, honey. No one here is surprised to see this rekindle with you and Mack." Then she sobered. "Is it serious, Darcy?"

Darcy sank down in the chair across from her and let her bag slide to the floor at her feet. "I don't know, Aunt Marla. There are so many reasons why it can't be, and yet..." She left the words unsaid.

"And yet it is anyway," Marla finished softly. Darcy could only nod. "Tell me again why you are fighting this?"

"You mean other than the fact that my life is in Chicago?" Was that her only reason?

Marla nodded. "Where's your heart?" She held up a hand before Darcy could speak, not that she had any answer for that question. "You don't have to tell *me*. You have to be honest with yourself. Go to him. Take some of that pie. And don't come home until morning."

Darcy was pretty sure her face was as red as the flaming red teakettle on the stove. "Yes, ma'am."

Marla drew her in for a hug when they both stood up. "We just want you happy, honey. That's all."

Mack had half expected Darcy not to show up. As it got later, and he looked at the damn clock every two minutes, he tried to convince himself he didn't care.

It wasn't true.

He'd checked on Fraser, who looked to be out of immediate danger but not out of the woods by a long shot. Jenn would check on him a couple more times before morning.

Another look at the clock. The cat sat on the back of the couch and cracked one eye halfway open when Mack leaned forward to check the time on his phone. Again. In case it was different than the time on the wall clock.

It wasn't.

He sat back with a *thump*, which finally dislodged the cat, who stomped over his lap on her way to the floor, where she sauntered off with a baleful flick of her tail.

This was stupid. He stared at the game on TV, not even caring what the score was, and usually he was glued to his alma mater's basketball games.

It didn't mean anything if she didn't come. It meant she didn't come and that was that. He was a big boy and could handle it. He knew she was wavering on the edge and so was he. Just because things had been good in the past didn't mean they'd be good now and all that. After all, they'd never dealt with the things in the past.

He almost had himself convinced she'd done them both a favor by not showing up when there was a knock on the door. He got off the couch as if he were rocket propelled, then forced himself to walk slowly to the door and ignored his stupid racing pulse.

It was Darcy, looking a little nervous as she worried her lower lip between her teeth. A lip he had every intention of kissing in the next few minutes. "Hi," he managed.

"Hi," she said, almost shy. She lifted a container.

"Marla sent pie. She caught me on my way out." Then she blushed.

Mack took the container and Darcy's arm and drew her inside. Something about the way she'd phrased that bothered him. "Caught you?"

The blush deepened as she unzipped her coat. "I went in the kitchen and she was there. I was hoping…" She trailed off and Mack's stomach dropped.

"You were hoping to avoid anyone knowing you are here?"

Her eyes widened. "No. I was hoping to avoid acknowledging what was going to happen when I came here. Even as an adult, it's an awkward thing to share with your relatives."

He pulled her in and kissed her, long and slow and deep. "And what's going to happen now that you're here?"

She plucked the container out of his hand with trembling fingers. "We're going to eat pie, of course."

With a laugh he followed her into the kitchen, watching as she greeted the dogs, who wagged at her as if she were a long-lost friend, before setting the dish down. He came up behind her and slipped his arms around her from behind and buried his face in her hair, like he used to do when they were dating, then married. She wrapped her arms around his and tilted her head so he could kiss her neck.

"Can the pie wait?" he whispered, and pressed against her backside, letting her feel his erection. She made him crazy and hungry and it wasn't for pie. She pressed back, making him groan her name, then turned in his arms.

"Make love to me," she whispered, and he had her

mouth, kissing her as if the whole world depended on it, before she could finish the last word.

They didn't make it very far, just out to the couch by the Christmas tree, and he'd managed to divest them each of their shirts and her bra by the time they got there.

With his hands full of Darcy's glorious breasts, he couldn't get her pants off, but that was okay because right now these needed his attention. He alternated between each sweet nipple with his tongue and his thumb, feeling her rise beneath him as she fumbled for the snap on his jeans. "Mack," she pleaded, and he shifted so she could get where they both wanted her to go.

When she tugged the zipper down and slid her hand into his boxers, closing around him, he groaned. "Darce," he panted.

A wicked smile curved her lips as her hand started to move up and down his length. "What?"

He'd forgotten. "Hell, honey—"

Her hand moved away and she started tugging on his jeans. "Off," she commanded, and he was more than happy to oblige. "Now sit and let me," she whispered. His erection throbbed and jumped and he fisted his hands in her hair as her hot mouth took him to the point the stars exploded around him.

It took him a minute to refocus and when he did, the only thing he saw was Darcy, kneeling between his legs, a smile on her face. Her breasts brushed the inside of his thighs as she leaned forward to get up. He caught her arms. "Your turn."

He had her pants down around her ankles and his mouth on her before she could do much more than gasp. She managed to get one foot out of her jeans and he lifted that leg up on his own thigh so he had better access to her. He wrapped his arm around her rear and held on as she braced her arms on his shoulders. She was so ready for him, so wet and hot, and she tasted like his own personal heaven. Her whimpers turned to cries as she reached her peak, and when she came apart he lowered her into his lap and drove himself home.

"Darcy," he growled, and she wrapped her arms around him, her breasts rubbing on his chest, and all that glorious friction and wetness and heat sent him right over the edge again, and by the contractions around him she was right there with him.

Spent, he lay back on the couch and arranged her next to him. "Wow," she breathed.

He pressed a kiss to her head. "Yeah. Wow." Clearly, they had no problems in the sex department. They never had. But it had never been that—explosive before. And it'd been plenty hot.

Chapter Fourteen

Sometime later, Darcy woke to feel Mack's fingers lightly stroking her flank. She blinked and lifted her head. He chuckled.

"Hey, sleepyhead."

She started to sit up and his hand came up to cup her breast. "Did I doze off?"

"We both did." He pulled her on top of him and took a nipple in his mouth, giving it a slow, lazy circle with his tongue. The tip of his erection pressed against her thigh. She adjusted so she could slide right down and take him all in. His hips rose to meet her and he let out a low groan.

This time they moved slow and sweet, and when the climax broke over her, he followed her over and held her while they floated back down, their bodies still joined. This wasn't sex. This was intimacy. That meant there were feelings involved.

Her stomach growled and he laughed. She lifted her head off his chest and managed a grin. "I guess it's time for pie."

It was a wonderful evening. They ate pie naked and talked—not about the past—and made love one last time, in his bed, before falling asleep. Her last thought, before she drifted off, was this was how it was supposed to be, all those years ago.

In the morning when she woke, Mack was gone, but she smelled coffee. Her clothes were neatly folded on top of the dresser, and her bag was on the floor in front of it. She stretched and couldn't help smiling at the slight soreness. They'd been busy and she'd loved every minute of it.

She got out of bed, took a quick shower, dressed and went in search of the coffee. There was a note on the counter.

Good morning, sexy. Had to go check on Fraser.
See you soon.

Not a lot, but it made her smile.

She poured the coffee into the mug he'd left out for her and patted the dogs, who seemed quizzical as to why she was still there. "It's okay, girls. I'll be on my way soon."

That was true in more ways than one, she knew. She'd be out of Holden's Crossing in a couple of weeks. And this would all be a wonderful memory. Much better than her last memories of her and Mack. They both deserved better.

It still meant she had to leave.

* * *

"Did you have a nice time, dear?" was all Marla asked when Darcy walked in the kitchen.

She held out the pie plate, trying not to picture her and Mack eating from it naked, feeding each other straight from the dish. Seemed very inappropriate here in her aunt's kitchen. "Yes."

"That's good." Marla turned to the chicken she was preparing. "Joe's going to go out to the barn tonight with you guys for a bit. Will you help me make sure he stays put and doesn't wander off to overdo it? You know your uncle. He'll want to 'check'—" here she used air quotes "—everything."

Darcy smiled, grateful the topic of her and Mack had been dropped. "Oh, yes. He will. Of course. We'll find a way to keep him busy." Her phone rang. A local number, but not one she knew. "Hello?" she said as she left the kitchen.

"It's Cheryl. Are you free for lunch today? I know it's short notice."

"I'd love that. When and where?"

Cheryl named a new café Darcy wasn't familiar with and they agreed to meet just before noon. That would give Darcy enough time to do some catching up with work emails and then be back in time for the evening's shift at the farm.

"So nice that you and Cheryl are reconnecting," Marla commented when Darcy told her her plans. "I was always so sad you let all those friendships go. Wasn't healthy for you to be so alone."

Darcy stood in the kitchen, her briefcase in one hand and her phone in the other. A stab of regret hit her hard. "I know. I just—couldn't do it. Be reminded." She'd had to bury her son and her marriage, too. It had been too much to hold. She'd been afraid that someone would tell her how Mack was doing and she'd never been sure what she'd been more worried about—that he'd be fine, or that he wouldn't be. Either one made no sense.

Marta laid her knife on the counter and wiped her hands on the dishrag. "I know. But you never allowed yourself to heal, Darcy. You closed it all off, but never let yourself work through the pain. It was too much for one person."

She didn't want to do this. Not now, not ever. "I'm fine."

Marla sighed and nodded. "I won't push. But let yourself feel, Darcy. You deserve to be happy. So does Mack."

Darcy slipped on her boots and walked out into the falling snow. Of course he did. They both did. But the only way she'd ever been able to really make him happy had been in bed. That hadn't changed, clearly, as they were combustible together. But didn't that mean they hadn't changed in other ways—and she hadn't been enough for him then. Why would now be any different?

Darcy pulled into the café's parking lot with five minutes to spare. She was looking forward to this, but a little nervous, too. She didn't want to blow it. She'd love to leave here with her friendship with Cheryl back on track.

Of course, she might have to come back sometimes for visits. But she wouldn't let that stop her. She could probably manage to avoid Mack, if it came to that.

They placed their orders with the cheerful girl behind the counter once Cheryl came in and greeted Darcy with a hug, as if they hadn't been apart for years. They chatted for a few minutes while waiting for their food, and once they were seated Cheryl asked the question that Darcy had been trying to figure out if she was going to bring up. "So. Tell me about Mack. Are you back together with him?"

"Ah." Darcy gave a little laugh and set her sandwich down. She hadn't even managed a bite. "No. Not really."

"*Not really* isn't an answer," Cheryl said slowly. Her expression was sympathetic. "What's going on, Darce? You don't have to tell me," she added quickly. "I understand."

Darcy gave up and filled her in, sparing no details except those of their actual lovemaking and ending with, "I'm not sure what to do. This isn't what I thought."

"No?"

She shook her head. "No. It's different this time. Not like, 'Oh, okay, we shared a past,' but more like—" She stopped, unsure of exactly what she wanted to say. Of what it meant.

"More like you share a future?" Cheryl said softly.

Darcy pressed her free hand to her eyes. "Yes." The word was a whisper.

"Oh, Darcy." There was a world of sympathy in Cheryl's voice. "What are you going to do about it? How can you make it work?"

Darcy thought of her job, her life in Chicago. That promotion was poised to take her to the next level, one she'd been working toward since she got there. How could she give that up? What would she do for income? She had savings, sure, but not enough to make that kind of life change. Did she even want to? "I don't know how. Or if it can be done."

"You love him." It wasn't a question.

"Yes." There was no point in denying it. "But what if it's left over from before, when we were married? How can I know it's real?" It felt real enough. But she just couldn't be sure.

"You know," Cheryl said simply. "You know you do. Trust yourself."

"There's one more thing," Darcy said quietly. "I didn't want to get married the first time. I was pregnant and he insisted. Not in a bad way or a mean way, just he really wanted to be married and start a family and all that. And I wasn't ready. I know it was too late to not be ready, cart before the horse and all that, but, Cheryl, I wasn't happy. I was freaking out and he thought it all was fine and wonderful." Now the tears were flowing, right there in the café, but she couldn't stop the words. "I didn't want any of it. Now, when I can't have any of it, I want it so badly it's tearing me up inside."

"Oh, honey," Cheryl said. She reached over and took Darcy's hand. "Did you tell him? Does he know that's how you felt, either then or now?"

"No," Darcy whispered. "I couldn't. He was so sure. I thought maybe there was something wrong with me, that I didn't want it, you know?" Mack hadn't known. He'd never guessed. Probably foolishly, she'd hid the truth from him instead of giving him the chance to help her. And he would have. He'd have moved heaven and earth for her if she'd allowed him the chance. But she hadn't.

"You need to tell him," Cheryl said firmly. "He needs to know, because that's a big part of why you left, correct? You have to set him straight because that's the only way you can really move on and start over. You both deserve the chance to know the truth and decide where to go from there. Don't make this decision for him, Darcy. It's not fair."

Even though her friend's words were spoken in a gentle tone, they still stung, because Cheryl was right. She'd made that decision for him, for them, once. She couldn't do it again.

She took a deep breath. "Okay. You're right. I will. Soon."

"Saw Darcy's car in front of your place yesterday," Chase said, and Mack rolled his eyes. "I'm not going to tell what I'm supposed to ask you. But I will ask— have you lost your mind?"

"No," Mack said, taking the phone off speaker. This wasn't going to be a good conversation for his staff to overhear. "I haven't." But he had had his mind blown several times last night with the incredible sex he'd shared with Darcy. That wasn't a detail he planned to share with anybody, especially not his big brother.

Chase blew out a breath. "You are a glutton for punishment, little bro. I can't save you from yourself."

"No, you can't," Mack agreed. "So back off and don't try. Let me do this."

"She'll hurt you."

No doubt. "I can handle myself, Chase. I know she's leaving. She does, too. It's fine." But deep down he knew that wasn't quite true. It wasn't that easy. It never had been easy with Darcy, and it hadn't changed. There was too much history between them, history they hadn't touched, to be anything more than temporary. Because then they'd have to really examine the past and frankly, Mack couldn't see that going anywhere good.

He also knew it'd have to be dealt with sometime.

He owed her a lot, and as much as he wanted her in his bed, he didn't want to be destroyed by her all over again.

He hung up after promising he'd meet Chase for lunch tomorrow and exacted a promise from Chase that he'd drop this thing with Mack and Darcy. It had been grudgingly given, and had taken some minor threats, but his brother had agreed.

He didn't want to be reminded it would end again. That she'd leave again. He knew this, felt the time slipping past him like water in a fast-moving stream and every bit as impossible to hold on to. But it made it awfully hard to stay in denial—his current happy place, though he wasn't stupid, knew he'd have to deal with it sooner rather than later—when people kept waving her leaving in front of his face.

Even though their intentions were good.

He couldn't help but hope that somehow they'd be wrong. And that was why this was so dangerous.

On impulse, Darcy stopped at the vet clinic after her lunch with Cheryl. She wanted to check on Fraser and frankly, see Mack. She called him from the parking lot, hoping she'd caught him at a good time.

"Hello?"

"Hi, Mack, it's Darcy."

"I know." There was a smile in his voice and she heard barking in the background. "What's up?"

"Are you on lunch? I was wondering if I could see Fraser. If it's no trouble." She held her breath. If he said no and saw her car out here, she'd feel silly.

"Sure. I don't really take a lunch, but I've got a few minutes. Are you close?"

"Yeah," she said. "I'll be there in a couple minutes."

When she walked in, he was behind the counter. Her heart gave a jump and she felt a bit of a blush as their night together flashed before her eyes. He wore jeans and a light blue button-down and she just wanted to melt into him.

This was bad. Even knowing what she did—that she loved him, still—it scared her.

He gave her a smile and she was glad there was no one in the waiting area to see her blush. "Hey," he said, and came around the end to drop a kiss on her mouth. Brief, but hot and way too public.

"Hey," she said back. She loved the kisses, darn it.

A tall blond-haired woman strode in from the back, looking at some papers in her hand. "Mack, are we out of the purple packages of the dog flea treatments? I thought— Oh," she said as she looked up, drawing out the word, her gaze flying to Mack, then settling on Darcy. "Hello."

"Jenn, this is Darcy. Darcy, Jenn. She's the other vet here. And yes, we're out of that for now. Sherry said they called this morning and are back-ordered. They can deliver Monday, I think it was. The notes are on the desk there."

Jennifer came forward, hand extended, papers tucked under her opposite arm. "Good to know. Thanks. So nice to finally meet you, Darcy. Mack talks about you a lot. Or as much as a guy will talk."

Darcy couldn't help smiling as Mack shifted uncomfortably beside her. "Jennifer."

She looked at him innocently. "What?"

He just shook his head.

"It's nice to meet you, too," Darcy said, and meant it. Mack rested his hand on the small of her back and steered her toward a door. "We're going to check on Fraser."

"All right. He told you about that?" Jenn said to Darcy, and she nodded. "It was awful. Just—awful."

"You told her about me?" Darcy asked once he'd closed the door behind them.

His jaw tightened. "She'd heard some rumors. She made some guesses."

She stopped and laid a hand on his arm. His muscles flexed under her touch and she slid her hand down to grab his hand. "Mack. Is that okay?"

He paused at another set of doors. "Yeah. I just don't want you to think I go around talking about you. Or us. Or our past. It's private."

"I know," she said. "I wasn't worried or mad." But he seemed embarrassed. A light went off in her head. "Did you date her, Mack?"

He pushed open the door. "No. Not really. We'd hang out, I guess you could say, but it was never a date situation."

She followed him through the doors. The light was dimmer here and the smell was defiantly hospital-like. She swallowed hard. He stopped at a cage where a big dog lay under a blanket.

Even in this light, and when it was clear the animal was asleep, she gasped. She could see the scars and cuts and what looked like burns on his head. Tears burned her throat. "Oh, Mack."

His face was grim. "You should see the rest of him. He's in bad shape. He's going to lose a front leg. I was hopeful, but it's not going to heal right. But I couldn't do it at the first round of surgery."

She touched the cage quietly, not sure if she'd wake

him if she made too much noise. He was sleeping, breathing even. Mack noticed. "You won't wake him. He's under right now. Helps with the healing and the pain."

"Who pays for his care?"

"There's a fund that people donate to for situations like this, when an animal needs serious help or when an owner can't pay the bill. Same with Minnie. We do fund-raisers to keep it going. That will cover some of it."

And he'd pay the rest. He didn't say it, but he didn't have to. She knew. She tucked herself into his side and wrapped her arms around his waist. He slid an arm around her and squeezed. She could hear the steady beat of his heart under her cheek and felt the warmth of his skin through his shirt. "You're a good man, Mack."

He went still. "Anyone would help out, Darce."

No, they wouldn't. But she let it go. And she knew now what she'd given up when she walked away. She'd been so, so shortsighted. Stupid. So she held on while she could, knowing she'd have to leave again, and they stood there, in the dimness, and watched Fraser sleep.

A *clang* from inside the clinic broke the spell. She stepped away and he let her go. She cleared her throat. "Well. I guess I'll let you get back to work. I'd like to see him when he's awake, if you think that'd be okay."

He slid his hands in his pockets and started walking toward the door. "Should be. Starting tomorrow, I'll keep him on pain meds, but not keep him under. I'll let you know."

"Thanks." Darcy hitched the strap of her purse up, but before she could take a step, he turned her to face him and kissed her. A real kiss, hot and deep. He pulled away.

"That's the greeting I wanted to give you," he whispered.

She blinked at him. "Well, hello, then."

A slow, sexy grin spread over his face. "Hi."

"Thanks for the coffee this morning, by the way."

"You're welcome. Last night was amazing. Hands down the hottest night I've ever had."

Darcy was pretty sure her blush had spread to her toes. She swallowed hard. "Yeah. Me, too."

He kissed her again, a gentle one this time. "Thank you."

"For what?"

"For taking the chance to come over. I know it wasn't easy for you."

His gaze was gentle and saw too much. She wasn't ready to face that, to let him all the way in. So she just smiled back and followed him out of the ward and back into the clinic, where an older man sat with a cat carrier. The occupant was yowling with displeasure.

"Ah, Doc," the man said with a wry smile. "Yoda is awfully excited to see you." He winked at Darcy and she couldn't help smiling.

"I can hear that," Mack said drily. "I'll be ready for him a few."

"No problem. We're early." The man went back to his magazine.

Mindful of all the ears that were suddenly around them—she'd seen Jenn in one of the offices when they came back out, and voices came from somewhere she couldn't see—she turned to Mack and gave him a quick smile. "Thanks for letting me see him."

"You're welcome. See you at the farm later."

Darcy nodded and walked out into the bright sun, which reflected off the snow and made her sneeze. He'd always teased her about her sneezing in the sun.

Chapter Fifteen

Jenn was waiting for him when he went back to his office to grab a fast bite to eat. Mr. Franklin was early, and while Mack would get to him as soon as possible, he needed three minutes to wolf down a sandwich.

"Not now," he said as he pulled the sandwich from the bag he'd retrieved from the office fridge. "Please."

Jenn shook her head and ignored him as he'd known she would. "Mack. It's serious, isn't it." Not a question. A statement.

He chewed his ham sandwich, not tasting it. He swallowed and reached for the water bottle on his desk. "Just a lot of history."

She shook her head. "More than that. Lots of people have history. You've got chemistry and clearly the two of you still have feelings for each other."

Now he choked on the bread. "You got all that from a one-minute introduction?"

She looked at him straight on. "Yes. It's obvious, Mack. Not only from seeing you together, but the way you talk about her. Do something about it, even if it's just settle the past so you can move on. You're not over her."

"I'm over her." The denial was quick and sure. He was. He had to be. It'd been a long time. "But what happened was really awful, Jenn. For both of us."

"It must have been," she said quietly. "I know you lost a child."

So she did know. His child and his wife. His family. His future. He wasn't interested in replacing them. He couldn't. He threw the last of the sandwich away, his appetite gone. Jenn was right. Things from the past needed to be settled before Darcy left again.

He finished out the afternoon at the clinic, ran home to take care of his pets and change his clothes as well as grab another bite to eat. He drove out to the tree farm, anticipation building in his chest. Jenn wasn't too far off. He'd fallen right back into this. It had been way too easy.

Sure enough, Darcy was there. She turned when he came in and gave him a smile. Things were growing there, no doubt about it. What they were exactly was a whole nother story.

"Mack." Joe's voice caught him off guard and he looked over to see the older man sitting on a stool behind the register, Marla smiling behind him.

"Joe. Good to see you out here. Feeling better?"

"Yep. I can be out here for a while. Can't do the heavy lifting, though. Doc won't let me, and my girls are keeping a close eye on me." The words were grumpy, but there was a twinkle in his eye.

Marla patted his shoulder. "That's 'cause we want you around for a good long time, dear."

Mack chatted with them for a couple more minutes, then excused himself to go outside, pulling his gloves on as he went. He wanted to talk to Darcy, but didn't think she'd want him hunting her down under the watchful eyes of her aunt and uncle. Not that they weren't adults. But he knew she was a little nervous about all this, and bringing them into it wasn't going to help matters.

Marla caught Darcy as she was walking past the register. "As soon as Mack came in, he looked for you." Marla's voice was gentle. "As soon as he saw you, he relaxed. Darcy, that man is in love with you. What are you going to do about it?"

Her heart pinged painfully in her chest. What was she going to do? She was going to leave because there was no other option. "It's been a long time, Aunt Marla. Too long. And we never talked about our past."

"Then, you need to do that. Work it out and see where it goes."

Darcy shut her eyes. She already knew she had to do that. Her conversation with Cheryl had driven that home. "I know we need to talk. But there's nowhere it can really actually go."

Marla reached for the box of mini–candy canes. She scooped a handful into the bowl that sat next to the register. "That's just an excuse, honey. You can make this work if you want it to. So I guess the question is, do you want it to?" She held up a hand. "You don't have to tell me the answer. It's between you and him. I'm just trying to make sure you don't make a big mistake you'll regret."

Another big mistake, Darcy amended silently. She'd made a lot in a short time, and no matter how casual she'd kept it, or tried to, the fact was it was going to hurt when she left. But was it a mistake to leave? That was what she wasn't sure of.

"I'll keep it in mind," she said finally. "I understand and appreciate your concerns. I really do." She stopped short of saying she knew what she was doing, because frankly, it wasn't true. The whole thing had gotten away from her as soon as Mack kissed her the first time.

Marla gave her a quick one-armed hug, the bowl of candy canes in her other hand. "We love you. We want you to be happy. That's all."

Darcy managed a smile as Marla hurried away to get Uncle Joe back to the house. She put the box of candy away and took a couple of deep breaths, trying to get her bearings. *That man is in love with you.*

She shook off the thrill the words gave her. No, he was in love with who she'd been years ago. He didn't really know her now. She'd changed. *So has he.* They were getting to know each other now, too, but how could it be enough? Could she be sure?

He was buying this farm. Once she left it, there was no coming back to it. Not like this. Marla and Joe were heading to warmer pastures. There'd be nothing here for her, nothing but memories. The physical places would be gone. That meant there was no reason to come back, to be here.

If she walked away from Mack, it would be for good. She wasn't foolish enough to think they could stay in touch. The contact would open old wounds each time. She knew that for a fact. But after she talked to him, would he want to be with her?

* * *

Darcy went out and filled in in one of the warming sheds. She kept the fire going, and the coffee and hot cocoa ready. She answered questions about trees, and directed people to the proper areas for the type of tree they were looking for. At the end of the evening she banked the fire, cleaned the pots, swept the little cabin and set everything up to go the next day.

It was snowing pretty good when she came out, the kind that had been sifting for a few hours and had piled up about three inches. Then Mack came around the curve. He stopped in front of her and cocked an eyebrow. "Want a ride?"

"Sure." She walked around and climbed onto the ATV, and he executed a three-point turn to head back in. The rough ride jostled them together and she couldn't even pretend she didn't mind the press of his arm on hers, even if she couldn't feel his heat.

"Your aunt and uncle went back to the house already," Mack said. "He looked happy, Darce. It was a good thing for him to be out here."

"That's good." She brushed the snow off her arms and looked up as Mack pulled her in for a kiss.

"I've been waiting for that all evening," he said, resting his head on hers. She leaned into him, even knowing it wasn't a good idea. She just couldn't help it.

"Me, too," she admitted.

"Come home with me tonight," he said, then the corner of his mouth quirked up. "I can't cook you dinner, but I can spring for takeout."

She should say no. There were so many reasons why this was a bad idea. Too bad she couldn't remember them at the moment. "That sounds wonderful."

But the truth was she couldn't bring herself to stay away. One more night wouldn't hurt, right? One more night before she had to tell him the truth.

"Excellent. Will you ride with me or bring your car?"

She hesitated, but only for a second. "I'll follow you."

They went up to the house and Darcy went to pack a bag while Mack talked to Marla and Joe. She tried not to dwell on the weirdness of it all, but failed. She threw in a change of clothes and her toothbrush, then sat on the bed and took a deep breath.

Things had shifted. How, exactly, she wasn't sure. But she had the feeling she'd finally reached the point where she couldn't go back.

And that scared her.

The snow had picked up and the plows hadn't been out yet—four inches or so wasn't much in terms of a northern snowfall—but it was coming down pretty hard and the wind had picked up. She kept her eyes on the taillights of Mack's truck and both hands on the wheel.

The trip took twenty minutes instead of the usual ten, but she gave a sigh of relief when they parked at his house.

He got out and came over to her. "We can ride together to the diner," he said.

"Okay." She gathered her keys and purse and left her bag on the backseat.

His truck was warm and smelled spicy, like him. Wonderful, like him. She buckled in and pulled her gloves off. He put it in Reverse and they drove the few minutes to the diner in silence. The lot was nearly empty, and they hurried in, the snow falling fast and hard.

"What can I get you?" The waitress wasn't the same one they'd had before. She was older, but friendly.

"Looking to place a take-out order," Mack said while Darcy scanned the menu quickly.

"Are you closing early?" she asked.

The waitress, whose name tag said Denise, nodded. "Night like this, we don't get much business."

They placed their orders and waited for the food. It didn't take long. Even in the fifteen minutes they'd been inside, there was significant snow to brush off the truck.

He pulled in the driveway next to her car, since with the plows it wasn't a good idea to park in the street. She opened the back door, got a bunch of snow dumped on her for her efforts and pulled out her bag. Inside she stomped off her feet and laughed. "Wow. It's quite a night out there."

He kissed her, a hungry openmouthed kiss that had her dropping her purse on the floor to hang on to him. "Yeah. Hopefully, in here, too."

She gave him a smile, her body tingling all over.

He built a fire and she set the food out on plates she found in the kitchen. They sat on the couch and ate, the dogs looking on hopefully.

"Wow, I didn't realize how hungry I was until I started eating," she admitted, reaching for the ketchup for her fries, a treat she almost never had. And the ones from the Town Line Diner were still the best.

"I knew I was starving," he said cheerfully as he polished off another bite of his burger.

"Your mom not cook for you lately?" she teased, and took another fry. Heaven.

"It's all good," he said. "She brought a potpie the

other day. It's in the freezer. It makes her happy and saves me time. Win-win for both of us."

Darcy didn't remember her own mother. She'd left not long after Darcy was born and died a few years after that. She'd been raised by her father, and her aunt and uncle. She didn't think her mother would have been the type to fill her freezer with leftovers. But Marla was. So she didn't feel left out. But there was the occasional pang of sadness that she'd never know the woman who gave birth to her.

"I can see that" was all she said, and took a bite of her own burger, another splurge. "Mmm. So good. It'll be so hard—" She stopped, as she'd been about to say *when I go back*. But she could tell from the way Mack stiffened that he knew what she hadn't said.

"Hard to what?" His attention was on her now, not on the food.

So he wasn't going to let her off easy. "To go back to Chicago."

"Then, why are you going?"

She stared at her burger, so good a moment ago. "Because it's where my life is." That was true. But she was starting to worry it wasn't where her heart was. How did she reconcile those things? Could she?

"Is it?" he murmured. "Darcy. Why did you leave?"

She froze. "You know why I left. After—after everything it was pretty clear we weren't going to make it." Which was true, and had played a big role in her leaving. But it wasn't all of it.

"You didn't give us a chance," he said quietly, but there was a hard note in his voice.

She slapped her hand on her chest. "I didn't?" Then

she pointed at him. "You didn't, Mack. You went to your family and left me alone."

"You wouldn't let me in," he said. "You wouldn't talk to me or let me see you. You shut me right down."

She shook her head. "That's not what I did, Mack. It's not."

He looked at her over the plates and stood up. He walked away, down the hall, and she heard him open a door. Should she leave? A glance out the patio doors showed the snow still coming down pretty hard.

Mack came back out in the living room with two boxes stacked in his arms. Darcy put her wineglass down and stood. "What are those?" She asked the question, but she knew the answer already. *Mack and Darcy, Christmas* was written on the tops in his mother's neat script.

He set them down carefully and looked at her solemnly. "My mom kept these. She packed it all up. After—after everything." Her heart started up as he opened the first one. "Look."

She set the glass down and the liquid sloshed around because her hand was so unsteady. She came over near him and saw ornaments from their first tree. Her breath caught. "Oh. Oh, Mack."

She touched the glass balls on top. The memories hit her hard, ones she'd tried so hard to keep at bay. She and Mack choosing these ornaments—none of them particularly special or expensive, but they'd had fun picking them out. That trip had, of course, ended in the bedroom and they'd wound up decorating the little tree in their apartment nearly naked, with Mack constantly touching her pregnant belly. She'd been six months along and had enough of a bump she'd just started wearing maternity clothes. He'd loved her pregnant body.

He'd loved her.

She swallowed. "What do you want to do with them?"

"We can put them on the tree," he said quietly. "Or we can divide them up and you can take them home."

Tears blurred her vision. That had been such a magical time. Not that they could ever really re-create it, but maybe they could use it as a new start. For something.

"Let's put them on the tree," she said when she found her voice. "They should be used."

He put on a Christmas station, and the festive tunes helped alleviate the pain she held in her heart. This would be fun, but bittersweet. Because he'd have to take them off the tree. Alone. After she'd gone. Like he'd had to the first time she'd left.

She pushed the thoughts aside and lifted out the first box. These were four chili peppers, because he loved spicy salsa. She couldn't hide her smile. "Remember these?"

He looked up from the other box and smiled. "Yeah."

It was easier than Darcy had thought to go through the boxes. Mack kept her laughing and sometimes he kissed her. But she caught him looking at her in that way, the way he used to, back when he loved her.

Marla's words echoed in her head. *That man's still in love with you.*

It wasn't possible. Was it? How could that be, after all this time?

She picked up a glass ball, hand-painted with the words *Darcy and Mack, First Christmas* with a heart and the year of their marriage. She froze, and held it in her hand. Did this go on the tree? Or did she try to bury it in the box?

She sent a furtive glance at Mack. He was looking in the other box, not paying attention. She could just tuck it in the tree, where it wouldn't be visible. She slipped it around the side and hung it deep in the branches, where it couldn't be seen if you were just walking by or sitting on the couch. When she came back over, he'd returned from the other side of the tree.

Mack's phone rang and he answered it with an apologetic look at Darcy. She smiled at him to let him know it was okay, and wandered over to check out the snow. The wind was howling now, banging against the windows. Peeking out the door, Darcy could see by the porch light the snow was really piling up. Several inches were on the porch, and her car was a white lump. She clearly wasn't leaving tonight. Not that she'd planned to, but it was always in the back of her mind. An escape plan in case things got to be too much, she supposed.

She went back to the tree and sat on the couch, just looking at it, now that it held their ornaments. It made the tree more theirs. She could hear Mack's voice in the kitchen. The dogs snored in front of the fire. The cat was asleep on the couch, too. It was cozy. Comfy. And she was content. This could have been her life. So different from her life in Chicago.

Mack came back and sank down next to her. "Sorry about that. Jenn was checking in. Normally, we don't do that unless there's a patient we are watching closely. In this case, Fraser."

"And how is he?" She didn't protest when Mack took her feet, one at a time, and pulled them into his lap.

"Making progress. He's got a long way to go, but

he is healing. Barring a serious infection, I think he'll make it. And I'm doing my damnedest to keep infection at bay. He doesn't deserve any less."

"I agree," she said softly. "What will you do with him when he's healed?"

He started to massage her foot. She scooted down a little closer. "When he's well enough he'll go to the shelter. They'll take care of him and see if he's adoptable. There's a list of people who will take him, but if any of them are suitable or if he's going to be able to be adopted is another matter."

"If he's not?"

Mack sighed. "I'll take him. Or find a home. He's terrified of people, thinks we're going to hurt him."

Her heart caught. "Of course he is. Poor guy. Any luck on finding who did it?"

"Actually, yeah. There's a promising tip that came in they are checking out. Hopefully, it pans out and they can make an arrest." He tugged her socks off and dropped them on the floor. She flexed her toes and propped a pillow under her head. They said nothing for a long while as they sat there in the light of the tree and listened to the crackling of the fire. Darcy found herself dozing. She couldn't shake the feeling that she was home.

Chapter Sixteen

When Darcy nodded off, Mack just sat and watched her for a few minutes. He wanted her, to be sure. But right now what he felt was more tender. He just wanted to keep her here, in this house he'd bought for them, in the little cocoon they'd spun tonight. Sure, it wasn't reality and he knew that all too well. But damn if she hadn't slipped right back in his life, as if she'd never been gone.

She stirred and he squeezed her leg. "Hey, sexy. Let's go to bed."

She sat up, sleepy eyed, and gave a big yawn. "Okay."

She got her bag and he heard her in the bathroom, as he banked the fire and unplugged the tree. It looked right now, with their ornaments on it. Then he went into the bedroom as she came out of the bathroom. Flannel bottoms, a long-sleeve T-shirt. No bra, as he could see her breasts sway gently as she moved. He gave her a slow smile. "Flannel? I'll keep you warm."

Her nipples peaked against the shirt and he took that as a yes. "Unless you're too tired."

She shook her head and he kissed her, long and slow. He was in no hurry. None at all.

It didn't take long to get her out of her pajamas—she was bare under the bottoms, too—and he took his sweet time with her body before finally sinking into her. They moved slowly and he never took his eyes off hers, even when her eyes blurred and she rose with her climax. When he followed her and collapsed on top of her, he knew this had been different. Something had changed. He rolled off her, then tucked her against him. She kissed his arm and he buried his nose in her hair as he pulled the blankets over them both.

Something had changed, all right. He was afraid he knew exactly what it was.

They made love once more in the night, and in the morning before he went to the clinic. Mack figured it was a great way to spend the night and start the day. In fact, he'd happily do it every day.

The snow hadn't stopped, but it had tapered off. There was a good foot of new stuff on the ground. Their vehicles were just white mounds. He went out through the garage and shoveled quickly—it was light and fluffy, so it didn't take too long to get it out of the way. Then he brushed off both his truck and her car and got in. This was why he had a four-wheel drive truck, he thought as he plowed his way down the street. They were last in line for the plows, being a residential neighborhood, so if he wanted to get anywhere on days like this, it was four-wheel drive and a steady hand.

It took him nearly three times as long as usual to

make the trip to the clinic, but he got there. He figured there'd be plenty of canceled appointments today.

Jenn was in the back when he walked in. "You made it" was her greeting.

"Ha. Yeah. No school today, I take it."

"Not according to the news, no. Do we want to call off any of the techs for today?"

Mack hesitated. "No, but tell them there's no rush. If they can't get here safely, then tell them not to risk it. We'll be okay today."

"All right." She gave him the report on the animals and went to call the techs while he went to see Fraser.

He looked at the big dog in the cage, who looked back at him with pain and fear and suspicion. He talked to him quietly. Jenn had already done the morning's meds. He'd change the bandages later when the meds had a chance to take effect. He made a point of talking to him quietly several times a day to try to win the dog's trust, or at least let him know Mack wasn't going to hurt him. He was very careful to avoid sudden moves and loud noises, as well.

It'd take time.

He went back up front as Jenn was hanging up the phone. "All done. They both said they'll try it but promised not to take chances. I don't think either of them will be here before ten."

"That's fine." He wondered when Darcy would attempt to go home. Would she stay? He hadn't asked her to, but not because he didn't want her to. It was because he wondered what she'd say.

Plus, asking her to stay sounded needy. He wanted her to do it—or not—because it was what she wanted.

Sure enough, almost all of the patients canceled. But

they still had a couple discharges to do today, and those people came in for their animals. Jenn went home for lunch and Mack sat behind the desk, looking over supply orders. This was the techs' job and they did it well, but since they weren't here, he figured he'd do it. When the bell on the door jingled, he looked up.

It was Darcy.

He rose as she plopped a huge bag of cat food on the floor at her feet and slapped one of the tags from his tree on the counter. Then she smiled. "Here you go."

He came around the counter and pulled her into his arms, allowing himself a deep kiss, which she happily gave. "Thanks," he said.

She stood there for a minute in his embrace. "I've got lunch, too. Let me go get it."

"You didn't have to—"

"It's not fancy," she laughed. "Hold on."

He transferred the cat food bag to the room he kept that stuff in. They made regular runs to the shelter and dropped items off. She came back in, a whirl of snow coming with her, and held up a bag. "Where do you want this?"

"Let's go in my office." He led the way and she followed. When she opened the bag, she pulled out sandwiches and fruit and chips. From another bag she took out two pops and offered him one.

"This is a nice surprise," he said. It was. It was wonderful to see her in his space, spending time with him. Just being together.

She gave a little shrug. "I just thought it'd be nice to have lunch together."

They chatted and finished. Then he asked her if she wanted to see Fraser and she said yes.

The dog gave a thump of his tail when he saw them, which was the first time he'd done that. She gave a little inhale. This time there was no blanket covering him. All his cuts and scars were out in the open. "Oh, Mack. Oh. You poor thing," she said to the dog, who shut his eyes and gave a little huff. She turned to look at Mack. "He looks awful."

"He's had it rough," he agreed, and that was an understatement.

"Are the circles cigarette burns?" she asked, and there was anger in her tone.

Fraser whimpered.

"Easy," Mack said to both of them. "Watch your tone. He's really sensitive to tone." No surprise given the abuse.

"Of course. Sorry, puppy," she said to the dog, who relaxed again, apparently not sensing any danger from them. "Heartbreaking. Sickening, too," she said to Mack, who nodded.

"That pretty much sums it up." He just hoped they'd find who did it, and soon. Fraser deserved nothing less than justice and a good home. A lot of animals in his situation got neither.

Darcy left for her aunt and uncle's after promising she'd be careful.

"I drive in snow," she pointed out. "We get our fair share in Chicago."

He knew that. But the accident still lingered with him after all these years. He'd never forget seeing her, banged up and bleeding and broken in that hospital. Ever. It was the moment his heart had stopped. "Just be careful. Please."

She gave him a kiss as Jenn walked into the room. With a quick greeting to Jenn, she was out the door.

"You have to tell her if you haven't already, Mack," Jenn said quietly. "She deserves to know."

"Tell her what?" Mack wasn't keeping anything from her.

"That you love her."

Mack shook his head, but he was afraid Jenn was right. "Jenn."

"Mack. You let her go once. Are you going to do it again? Because she's going to leave without knowing. How can you do that?"

Easy. If she left without knowing how he felt about her, he didn't have to run the risk of having his heart punted back at him. Again. The first time had been hard enough. He wasn't going to risk it again.

So he said nothing and Jenn sighed. "Mack. Don't be stupid."

"I'm not," he said. "I'm smart enough to know how this ends."

"Do you?" Her voice was quiet. "How can you be sure, if you haven't asked her?"

I don't have to ask her. No, she'd left once. That was enough for him. If she wanted to stay, she would. She'd find a way. But he couldn't risk rejection anymore. This time would kill him for sure. He just shook his head.

She sighed but left it alone. For that he was grateful.

Darcy made it to the farm. It took a while, but she got there, snow and all. The main roads had been plowed but were still tricky. The lane to the farm had been plowed as well, but the packed snow was still slippery. Her SUV was designed for this. Probably why she'd bought it, even in Chicago where she relied mostly on mass transit—she'd gotten so used to vehicles with four-wheel drive that it hadn't occurred her not to purchase one for herself.

Ironic that back here was where she needed it the most.

She parked and hauled her bag out of the backseat. Joe had a checkup with the heart doctor today, so her aunt and uncle weren't there. Luckily, they didn't have to drive far for it. She was kind of relieved that she didn't have to come in with her bag after an overnight at Mack's.

But last night had been different.

She was trying not to dwell on it, but something had shifted. What that was, she couldn't quite pinpoint. She did know she needed to tell him what had really happened, and she needed to tell him tonight.

The nerves wouldn't quit.

The farm was open, even in the snow, and Mack was everywhere. Darcy was jumpy and distracted all evening. Marla kept giving her strange looks, but she managed to stave off any questions because they were so busy. She kept rehearsing what she wanted to say in her head. Running through it over and over.

It didn't help.

Finally, when it was all said and done, she went up to Mack, whom she'd been somewhat avoiding all evening, torn up by guilt and nerves. "Do you have time to talk?"

Clearly, he'd picked up on her tension, because he looked at her closely. "Darcy. Are you okay?"

She hesitated, then nodded. "But we need to talk," she repeated.

"All right. Can we go back to my place? I need to check on the dog." He was looking at her with concern.

It took about fifteen more minutes to close down, say good-night and get everyone out the door. Darcy's nerves had taken the form of huge angry butterflies in her stomach. She followed him to the clinic, where she stayed in her car, then to the house. By the time they got there, she was ready to explode. Was it the right thing? To tell him, after all these years? Did it matter anymore?

Yes. It did matter.

"What's going on?" His voice was quiet once they got in the house and the dogs were wagging around them. She saw the concern in his eyes, but he didn't reach for her. Clearly she was giving off stand-back vibes. "Darcy."

She took a deep breath and looked at him, at this man she loved so much. Always had and, she suspected, always would. "I wasn't ready to get married," she blurted. "I wasn't ready for any of it." She put her hands over her eyes. That was the easy part of the truth.

He moved closer but still didn't touch her. "What do you mean?"

It was so important she make him see. "You were so sure. *So sure*, Mack. Of yourself. Of us. Of everything. And I went along because I wanted to be sure, too."

"Why didn't you say anything?" He sounded shocked, as if it had never occurred to him. Maybe he hadn't noticed the change in their relationship after they'd gotten married. She'd tried so hard to hide it.

She laughed, but it was more of a sharp bark than a joyful sound. "I was pregnant, remember? We had to get married. I thought maybe some of your optimism would rub off on me, too."

He just looked at her, his face unreadable. She forged on. "And again, you are so damn sure you know what's best here, too. Buying the farm, making it into something you know I'd never want it to be."

She drew a shaky breath. "I loved you then, Mack. So much. But you didn't feel the same, after all that sureness. You let me walk away."

"Come with me." He didn't offer her a hand, but stalked off down the hall, and she followed after a moment. He went into the room that usually had the door shut. It had some boxes stacked up. Clearly, he used this one for storage. He opened the closet door and took out a couple of boxes labeled—

Oh, God.

Labeled *Baby.*

She wanted to back away, but couldn't make herself move, much less look away. "Where have those been?"

"My mom held on to them."

Of course she had. If she'd held on to the ornaments, she'd hold on to the baby stuff. Behind him, in the closet, she saw a long box. Her heart stopped. "Mack. What is that?"

He moved out of the way, his jaw set, his arms crossed over his chest. "Look. Look at all of it, Darcy."

It was the crib. They'd bought it two days before the accident. Had never had the chance to open it, much less set it up. He didn't move when she pressed her hand to her mouth and laid the other on the box. She couldn't speak.

"Look in the others," he said, his voice rough.

She did. She moved from the crib, her hands shaking so badly she almost couldn't open the next box. But she managed and couldn't stop the tears. More baby stuff. Things they'd picked out together. Blankets, onesies, the changing table. Crib bedding, printed with trains. Not to mention their wedding china and other assorted gifts that he'd never used. All of it, he'd held on to for all these years. She finally sank to the floor and sobbed. All of it, the pain, the regrets, the truth spilled free. And then Mack was behind her, pulling her in and she felt his own tears on her hair. She wrapped around him and burrowed in, the sobs shaking them both. He stroked her hair and finally her sobs reduced to hiccups.

He just rested his head on hers and held on. He didn't ask if she felt better, which was good because no, she didn't. She really, really didn't. She felt worse. She'd assumed he'd gotten rid of all this stuff. Let it all go, the pieces of their old life that never really got started. But here it was, their old life, real and tangible and oh-so-painful.

"Mack," she whispered finally, and he said, "What?"

She pulled away and looked at him. His eyes were red rimmed and her heart ached because she wasn't done delivering the blows. "I'm so sorry. For all of it. For causing the accident—"

"It was an accident, Darce. You didn't do anything."

She lifted her chin. It was time he knew. "I did. I turned left instead of right because I was delaying coming home." At his confused look she faltered, her stomach twisting in knots, then forced herself to continue. He deserved to know the truth. "I can't stress this enough. You were so sure, Mack. So sure of us, of the baby, of our future. Everything. But I wasn't. We got married because of the baby. And then it was gone and with it, the whole reason for our marriage."

He sat there, stunned, and stared at her tearstained face. "What do you mean, the whole reason for our marriage?"

"I wasn't ready to get married, much less be a parent. I thought maybe it'd get better. I knew I was going to have to figure out parenting. But the marriage…" She trailed off, looking lost.

"But the marriage, what?" His voice didn't sound like his own. It seemed to come from far away.

She swallowed hard. "I was going to see if we could separate."

Her words couldn't have hit him any harder if she'd shot him. He gaped at her. "Separate? You wanted to leave me? While you were pregnant?" What the hell was this? How had he missed it?

Her face was ghostly pale and her eyes were full of pain. And guilt. "Yes. I wasn't thinking straight and it was an impulsive decision. So I turned left and—" Her voice caught, and then she continued, "And the other car was there. I didn't see it because I was trying to make the light."

Which had been yellow and she'd broken no laws. The other car had run the light and hit her broadside. He wasn't fully tracking here. She'd wanted to leave him. That had been her plan all along.

Then it hit him. "You had no intention of ever staying," he said slowly. "Not then. Not now. All this was just for, what? Show? Pity?" Anger filled him, white hot, and that was better than the equally strong pain that was trying to push through.

She touched his leg and he pulled back. He couldn't have her touch him. She affected him in ways—still— that wouldn't help him get over her. "Mack. Please understand. We were so young and I was scared and confused." There was a plea in her voice. He couldn't understand.

He looked away. She couldn't have talked to him about it? Was he that awful? Had he been that bad a husband? He didn't remember their marriage being awful. Yeah, she'd been a little nervous, but weren't all new parents-to-be? Clearly, he hadn't known her as well as he'd thought.

"And now?" He waited for her answer, knowing he wouldn't like it.

There was a long pause and he heard her breathing, which seemed so loud in the quiet room, almost as loud as the blood rushing in his ears. "Now I know better," she said finally, her voice sad and low.

He couldn't move. She'd left him once, and it had nearly killed him. And here she was, leaving again, without giving their future any thought.

He hadn't learned. All these years, and he hadn't freaking *learned*.

After a moment, she stood up and left the room without a word. He was pretty sure there was nothing left to say. He heard the front door close shortly after that. It was pretty clear—she'd never felt for him what he had for her. He remembered his mother's words—she hadn't been ready. He'd waved her off, but it seemed she'd been right after all. Darcy would never be ready. Not for what he had to offer.

He got up off the floor and left the room and pulled the door shut, not bothering to close the boxes that were open and all over the floor. They didn't matter now. They were part of a life that hadn't ever really existed, apparently.

What a fool he'd been.

Chapter Seventeen

Mack moved through the next day in a fog. Jenn gave him worried looks, but didn't ask any questions. He didn't go out to the tree farm. He wasn't sure he had it in him to act as if everything was okay. So when his brother showed up to take him to grab a beer, he didn't have the energy to turn him down.

Chase booted up his laptop once they were seated. "Been making plans for the new sub. Want to see?"

He really didn't want to see it, or have anything to do with anything Darcy related right now. Mack stared at the screen when Chase turned it to face him. "This is Darcy's farm?"

"No," Chase said slowly. "Darcy left. This is Joe and Marla's farm. That they are going to sell to us after the holidays. Remember?" He looked at Mack. "Ah, shoot. You did it, didn't you?" He swore.

"Did what?" Mack asked, his gaze back on the computer screen. Chase had left a lot of trees and had carved out large home sites. It'd be gorgeous. Darcy would hate it. The thought gave him no pleasure.

"You fell in love with her."

His gaze flew to Chase's. Actually, it was more accurate to say he'd never stopped loving her. "She's out of here in a few days." She'd been crystal clear there was no hope of a future. She hadn't wanted one back then. She didn't want one now. Then again, he hadn't asked her, had he? He'd been more than happy to have her company, both in bed and out of it. He'd been afraid if he'd asked for more, she'd bolt.

Of course, as it turned out, she was going to bolt anyway, so it wasn't as if he'd saved himself any grief, now, had he?

"Clearly, that doesn't matter." Chase took the laptop back and closed it, slipping it into his bag. "I noticed you didn't deny it. So. What are you going to do now?"

"Nothing. Like I said, she's leaving." The words were bitter in his mouth. He took a deep draw of his beer to try to erase the picture of her tearstained face.

"You're a coward," Chase said flatly.

Mack's head snapped up and he barked out a laugh. "What? Why? You've been telling me all along to let her go. To not get involved." He could not win.

"And you did neither of those things," Chase pointed out. "You *can't* let her go and you *are* involved and not in the kind of way that will allow her to walk away from you without ripping out your heart. So." He leaned on the table, looked Mack in the eye and threw down the gauntlet. "I repeat. You're a coward. What the hell are you gonna do about it?"

Mack opened his mouth, then shut it again. "You're an ass. You know that, right?"

"Yeah, thanks. But it doesn't solve your problem."

Chase was right. Mack didn't really want to acknowledge it to his brother, much less himself. Still, denial hadn't served him so well. He let out a breath. "I'm not being a coward if I let her go. She wants to go. Why would I fight that?"

"But you want her to stay," Chase pointed out quietly. "And you're going to let her walk. That's gonna suck for you. So why not try? At this point, what do you have to lose?"

A lot, actually. If he took a stand and she left anyway, it'd be too damn hard. Chase was right. He wasn't willing to risk the pain. "She's going to leave anyway."

Chase shook his head. "How do you know? Have you given her a reason to stay? No," he answered himself. "You haven't. I don't get this. I understand not wanting to get hurt, because that sucks. But you've got a second chance with the woman you love and you are letting her go without a fight."

Mack hadn't been enough the first time around. Why would now be any different?

He rubbed his hand over his face. "I can't explain it, okay? She hasn't given me any hint she's willing to give it another shot."

"No? She's in your bed, am I right? You rearranged your whole schedule to be out at the farm more. She looks at you the same way you look at her, with that sappiness couples in love have. It's all there, Mack. If I can see it, you damn well should be able to." Chase leaned forward. "Go. Talk to her. Fix this, Mack. For both of your sakes."

Mack just stared at his brother. He wasn't sure what to say. Chase had been so adamant that he stay away from Darcy. Not that Chase had any control over Mack's life, but he knew how bad it had been for Mack in the aftermath and had been trying to keep that from happening again. "Why are you doing this?"

Chase rose from the table and picked up his laptop bag. He put money on the table to cover his bill. "Because you should be happy. Think about it," he said, and slapped Mack on the shoulder as he went past him.

Happy. Darcy had made him very happy, until she'd left him. But he hadn't made her happy. Was Chase right? He hadn't tried hard enough to see what she was feeling? She'd lost so much—they both had. He didn't even care if she was infertile. There were lots of ways to make a family. In retrospect he could see that he hadn't handled everything so well. All he'd wanted was for them to be happy. In trying to give her space, he'd pushed her away.

They'd both made mistakes. But the question was— was it too late to fix them?

Marla called up the stairs, "There's someone here to see you, Darcy."

Darcy frowned at the laundry she was folding. "Be right down," she called back. If it'd been Mack, Marla would have said so. But it wouldn't be him, not now. Not since she'd told him the ugly truth. She'd handled it poorly, to be sure. She'd run when she should have tried to make him see. The look on his face when he'd shut down—she shivered at the memory. He'd never looked at her like that. As if she were a stranger.

She came downstairs and stared at the man in the

kitchen. Chase. She hadn't been expecting to see him, either.

Marla folded the dish towel and hung it over the stove handle. "Nice to see you again, Chase." She gave Darcy's arm a little squeeze as she left the room.

"Um, hi," she managed. Chase had been decidedly unfriendly to her over the past weeks, clear in his anger over her treatment of Mack all those years ago. She'd never blamed him, had accepted it as her due. "Have a seat," she suggested, and started toward the table. Chase shook his head.

"No, thanks. This will only take a minute." He looked at her, and she could see his mistrust of her hadn't abated, but there was resignation in there, too.

"Okay," she said slowly, curiosity almost getting the better of her. But she waited for him to speak.

"Are you leaving?"

"Yes," she said slowly.

He nodded. "Mack is in love with you. Still. Hell, he'd kill me if he knew I was here. I don't know what you feel for him, if you ever loved him. You left him behind awfully easily."

"It wasn't easy," she shot back. It'd been so hard. So. Hard.

"You left him," Chase repeated. "Is this time going to be different?"

"What do you mean?" His words were starting to sink in. *Mack is in love with you.* Chase would probably know that. More than anyone else. He and Mack had always been close. Her heart gave a little flutter.

He looked her in the eye. "You know what I mean," he said quietly.

She lifted her chin. "That's my business."

"I disagree. It's Mack's, too. Fix this for both of you or he'll be the wreck he was when you left the first time."

"Wreck?" He hadn't tried to contact her after the divorce. They'd communicated only through lawyers. It had only served, at the time, to reinforce she'd done the right thing.

"Yes. A wreck. Now you're going to walk away. Again. And leave him to pick up all the pieces. Why?" He turned to go. "I'm not the one who needs the answer to that question. But if you love my brother, you'd better figure this out quick. I don't think you'll get a third chance."

She didn't want a third chance. She hadn't been sure she should have a second chance. She stood for a moment, heard the door close, then an engine start.

Chase was right. She had to do something, something to fix this.

She hurried out into the living room, where her aunt and uncle were watching a Christmas movie on TV and Marla was knitting. "I'm going into town."

Marla frowned in concern. "Now? It's so late."

"I know. It's important." More important than anything.

"All right," Marla said. "Are you going to see Mack?"

She didn't hesitate. "Yes. Yes, I am."

Her aunt and uncle exchanged smiles. "Good for you," Marla said at the same time Joe said, "'Bout time."

Darcy took the stairs two at a time, grabbing her purse and keys and running back down. She didn't know what kind of reception she'd get. Or if he'd even be home, actually.

She knew exactly what she was going to do. It was all so clear, and felt completely right.

* * *

She drove as fast as the conditions allowed, but once she got there and parked in front of the house, she sat for a moment. She'd been trying to rehearse what to say to him, but nothing really stuck. Now, in front of the house, seeing the dark shape of the tree they'd picked out and decorated, her heart squeezed.

She'd been so wrong. So afraid. And she'd taken it out on him.

She got out of her car and took a deep lungful of the cold, still air. All around were houses all decked out for the holidays—trees in windows, twinkle lights on trees and houses and bushes. But this one—this one was dark.

She walked up the drive to the front door and knocked.

After a moment the door opened. Mack stood there, silhouetted against the frame. She linked her fingers to keep them from shaking. "Can I come in?"

In answer, he stepped out of the way and she came in, closing the door behind her. He went and sat back on the couch, arms crossed. So he wasn't going to make this easy. That was okay. It shouldn't be easy.

She perched opposite him on a chair, her back to the tree and the window. She unzipped her coat but didn't take it off. He muted the TV and gave her his full attention, but she couldn't read his expression. She took a deep breath. "Mack. I'm so sorry. I really handled this wrong." It was an understatement and didn't really cover the depth of her feelings.

He leaned forward and rested his forearms on his knees. He was wearing gym shorts despite the cold temperature outside. "Me, too."

That stopped her in her tracks. She frowned. "You? How did you?"

"I didn't pay close enough attention, then or now. You weren't wrong. I was pretty sure of myself. Of us. Too sure." He gave her a pained grin. "I didn't mean to be overbearing, Darce. I just thought—I just thought it'd all kind of work out on its own."

That little flutter of hope grew into a flare. She took a chance and moved next to him on the couch. He didn't move away. "I should have talked to you, told you what I was feeling, instead of hiding it from you. And I should have come home long before now to apologize." Of all of it, that was what she regretted the most. She'd let so much go—not just Mack, but her friendships here in town, and let her aunt and uncle down, too. All because she'd been unable to face her feelings.

"Darce." There was a tenderness in his voice now that made her eyes burn. He ran his hand along her jaw and she turned her face into his palm. The heat of his touch made her want to burrow into him and never let go. Ever. "No apologies. We both screwed up. If I could go back, I'd ask you what was wrong and pester you until you told me. I won't make that mistake again."

She opened her eyes and looked at him, almost afraid to breathe. "What are you saying?"

"I love you. That's what I'm saying. I never stopped. I was going to ask you to stay, but I realized that's not fair. Jenn can run this practice with one hand tied behind her back. I can find a place in Chicago—"

"Wait." Her heart leaped with joy. In all that was one important point she needed to hear again. "You love me? Really?"

"Really." He pressed a kiss to her mouth.

"I love you, too," she whispered, and kissed him back, trying to pour all she felt into the kiss so he would know she'd never leave again. Just as his hands came up under her shirt, she eased back. "But. There's one thing you should know."

He eased back but kept his arms around her. "What's that?"

She took a deep breath. "I'm not leaving. I'm not going back to Chicago. Well, not for long anyway. I'm going to quit my job and move up here to run the tree farm."

Mack stared at her. "You what? You are?"

She nodded. "I haven't been happy there since I left here. Coming back here was coming home. You're here. My roots are here. And I want to make all that work." It had taken losing him—again—to make her see it and realize it.

He sat back. "Wow. Do your aunt and uncle know?"

She shook her head. "No. Not yet. I just decided. I know you guys wanted to buy it—"

"I think your aunt and uncle will be thrilled to sell it to you. I think that's part of why they wouldn't finalize the sale until after you left. They were hoping you'd take it over."

Sneaky of them, too. "I don't know how it all will work. You've got this adorable little house. I'd hate to move you out to the farm—I mean, if this is going anywhere…" She faltered. Was she getting ahead of herself? He pulled her in for another kiss.

"Oh, it's going, sweetheart. As soon as you're willing, I'm ready. I bought this house for us. Well, I found it and before I could tell you about it, the accident happened. But this is where I wanted to raise our son, and any brothers and sisters he might have had. After you left, I went ahead and finalized the sale and remodeled it. It's what saved my sanity."

Darcy stared at him, her jaw on the floor. She hadn't known he'd bought a house at that time. Or even that he'd been looking. She'd shut down at any mention of Mack and her aunt had eventually stopped bringing him up. It had been too hard.

"I— Wow. Mack. You bought this house for us?" Was that why it'd felt so homey to her? Tears gathered in her eyes, but this time they were happy tears. "Then, let's stay here."

"No rush to figure it out," he whispered against her neck. She laid a hand on his chest. He stopped and looked up at her, heat and exasperation in his gaze. "We're still talking?"

She had to laugh. "Yes. We are still talking. There's one more thing."

He sighed and trailed his hand up her side, over her breast, clearly with something else on his mind. "Okay. What's that?"

She hesitated. "I know you wanted more kids. And you know I most likely can't have them."

"Yeah."

"And?" She held her breath.

"And what?" He sat up and looked at her steadily. "There are lots of ways to make a family, Darce. We can adopt. Try fertility treatments if you want. Be foster parents. I'm open to anything."

The love she felt for him rose and nearly swamped her. She couldn't say anything, so she just nodded.

He kissed her again and pulled her in close. "Now are we done talking?" The words were a playful growl.

She laughed and wrapped her arms around his neck as he scooped her off the couch and started toward his bedroom. She pressed her face into his shoulder, closed her eyes and held on tight.

Oh, yes. She was definitely home.

* * * * *

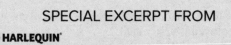
"Okay," Olivia said in a dejected voice. "Thank you for
bringing me down here to meet Sparkle and play with
the puppies."

"You are very welcome," Celeste said. "Any time you
want to come back, we would love to have you. Sparkle
would, too."

Olivia seemed heartened by that as she headed for the
reindeer's stall one last time.

"Bye, Sparkle. Bye!"

The reindeer nodded his head two or three times as if
he were bowing, which made the girl giggle.

Celeste led the way out of the barn. Another inch
of snow had fallen during the short time they had been
inside, and they walked in silence to where Flynn's SUV
was parked in front of the house.

She wrapped her coat around herself while Flynn
helped his daughter into the backseat. Once Olivia was
settled, he closed the door and turned to Celeste.

"Please tell your family thank-you for inviting me to dinner. I enjoyed it very much."

"I will. Good night."

With a wave, he hopped into his SUV and backed out of the driveway.

She watched them for just a moment, snow settling on her hair and her cheeks while she tried to ignore that little ache in her heart.

She could do this. She was tougher than she sometimes gave herself credit. Yes, she might already care about Olivia and be right on the brink of falling hard for her father. That didn't mean she had to lean forward and leave solid ground.

She would simply have to keep herself centered, focused on her family and her friends, her work and her writing and the holidays. She would do her best to keep him at arm's length. It was the only smart choice if she wanted to emerge unscathed after this holiday season.

Soon they would be gone, and her life would return to the comfortable routine she had created for herself.

As she walked into the house, she tried not to think about how unappealing she suddenly found that idea.

Don't miss
A COLD CREEK CHRISTMAS STORY by
New York Times *bestselling author RaeAnne Thayne,*
available December 2015 wherever
Harlequin® Special Edition books
and ebooks are sold.

www.Harlequin.com

REQUEST YOUR FREE BOOKS!

2 FREE NOVELS PLUS 2 FREE GIFTS!

◆ HARLEQUIN®

SPECIAL EDITION

Life, Love & Family

HSE15